The
SECRET
FATHER

HILDA STAHL

Accent Books™ is an imprint of David C. Cook Publishing Co.
David C. Cook Publishing Co., Elgin, Illinois 60120
David C. Cook Publishing Co., Weston, Ontario
Nova Distribution Ltd., Newton Abbot, England

THE SECRET FATHER
©1986 by Word Spinners, Inc.
Revised 1992

All rights reserved. Except for brief excerpts for review purposes, no
part of this book may be reproduced or used in any form without
written permission from the publisher.

Cover design and illustration by Terry Julien
First Printing, 1986
Printed in the United States of America
96 95 94 93 92 7 6 5 4 3

Library of Congress Catalog Card Number 86-70271

ISBN 0-78140-517-3

CONTENTS

1

HEATHER'S DEMAND

With one quick jerk, Wren zipped up her blue jacket, then ran to the end of the sidewalk to wait for Bess. Boys and girls streamed from the school shouting and laughing, glad that the day was over and they could go home. Just then Wren saw Tim Avery at the bike stand unlocking the ten-speed that Adam Landon had bought him. Tim's red hair stuck out as if he'd just pushed his fingers through it. With the October breeze blowing, he looked chilly wearing only a tan, long-sleeved pullover shirt and lightweight pants.

Wren took a step toward Tim, then stopped as a woman ran up to Tim and grabbed his arm. Tim looked around quickly, his face bright red. He saw Wren and glared at her as if to dare her to speak to him.

"What's with him?" she muttered, but she stayed where she was. It had taken them a long time to become friends, but now that they were, she wanted to keep it that way.

"Tim, you have to do it," Wren heard the woman say in

a sharp voice. "You know how important it is to me!"

Tim pulled away, shaking his head. "No, Mom! Don't make me!"

Wren's eyes grew big and round. This was Tim's mother, Heather Avery! "I can't believe it," Wren whispered. She had never seen Tim's mother. Tim had made sure that Wren never went inside his home and she knew it was because his mother was an alcoholic. Tim felt bad when his friends heard his mother yell at him or saw her passed out from drinking.

"Don't be this way, Timmy," Wren heard Mrs. Avery say with a pout.

"I said I wouldn't, and I won't!" Tim shook his head hard.

Wren bit her lower lip. What did Heather Avery want Tim to do? Wren had seen Tim upset before, but never like this. He looked ready to explode.

Heather caught Tim's arm again and shook him. Her face was as red as her tangled hair. Dark smudges lined her wide blue eyes. "I need you to get money from him, Tim, and you will do it!"

Tim shot an embarrassed look around before he lifted his face to his mother. "Don't, Mom! I won't go see him. I can't."

Just then Bess Talbot stopped beside Wren. "What's wrong?"

"Tim. His mother," whispered Wren.

Bess's eyes widened. "Is that his mother? Is she drunk?"

Wren frowned. "Shhh. Tim will hear you."

"He can't hear me. He's too busy with his mother."

Paula jabbed Wren in the back. "What's going on with Tim?"

Wren spun around. She hadn't noticed Paula Gantz walk up. Paula always stuck her nose in where it didn't belong. "Nothing is going on, Paula. Go spy on someone else."

"Spy? Me, spy?" Paula pushed her face close to Wren's. "You're the only spy around here, Wren House!"

"I do not spy! I do detective work!"

Paula tossed her brown hair. "You wish!"

Wren flushed and pressed her lips together in a thin, tight line.

Paula glanced over at Tim and his mother, then back to Wren. "Do you think this is another mystery to solve?"

"Is it a mystery?" asked Bess with a worried frown. The wind blew a strand of her blonde hair, and she hastily brushed it back in place.

"No. It's not," Wren answered. But she looked closer at Tim and his mother. Was it a mystery? It had been almost three weeks since she'd had a chance to do any detective work. Maybe she was losing the ability to sniff out trouble. She shivered at the terrible thought and took a step forward, but Bess caught her arm and tugged her back.

"It's none of your business, Wren House," said Bess in a firm voice.

Wren shook her finger at Bess. "You're too cautious, Bess! What if there is a mystery? What if Tim needs our help?"

"Well, I'm going to walk right up to them and say hello to Tim's mother," said Paula. "I couldn't hear the fight since you girls were arguing." Paula lifted her chin. Her skirt pressed against her thin legs as she marched forward.

Wren hesitated, then ran after Paula with Bess right behind her. They stopped in front of the Averys.

Paula looked right at Tim's mother. "Hello, Tim."

"Get away from me," snapped Tim. He tugged on his mother's arm. "Let's go home right now, Mom. I'll make you a sandwich and a cup of coffee."

She shook her head, then smiled at the girls. "Hello, girls. I'm Heather Avery, Tim's mother."

Wren stepped forward, smiling slightly. "I'm Wren House."

Heather Avery frowned. "Wren House? Are you teasing me?" She looked at Tim. "Is she teasing me?"

"No, she's not, Mom." Tim tugged Heather's arm again, but she shrugged him off.

Wren flushed. It was always the same when she said her name to a stranger. She hated telling that Mom had named her Wren House so no one would ever forget her name.

"Her mom named her," said Bess. "I'm Bess Talbot."

"And I'm Paula Gantz. My dad's a doctor. Where's Tim's dad?" Wren saw the look of pain that crossed Tim's face. She wanted to tell Paula to shut her mouth and leave it shut.

"Let's go, Mom." Tim's voice broke and he looked as if he was going to cry.

Heather leaned toward Paula. "Tim does have a dad, and he lives right here in Jordan City."

Wren bit back a gasp, and she heard the sharp intake of Tim's breath.

"Where does he live?" asked Bess, her face flushed with curiosity. "What's his name?"

Wren saw the color drain from Tim's face. She knew he thought his dad lived too far away to visit him. It was awful to think his dad lived nearby and didn't take the time to see Tim. Wren reached out for Tim, but the fierce look on his face made her drop her hand.

"I am going home, Mom," said Tim stiffly.

"Don't go yet," said Paula. "I want to know your dad's name." Paula looked up at Heather. "Do I know him?"

"Stay out of this," snapped Tim. He turned to his bike. "I'm going home right now, Mom. I will not go ask for money! I mean it!"

"We'll talk at home, Tim Avery!" Heather spun on her heels and strode down the walk while Tim jumped on his ten-speed and pedaled away.

Paula let out her breath in a whistle. "Who is Tim's dad? I'm going to look in the phone book for Avery and call everyone until I find his dad."

Wren bit her lip to keep from saying that the only other Avery in the phone book was an old woman not related to Tim. She'd learned that when she'd tried to call him.

"I want to know who Tim's dad is, too." Bess stamped her foot. "And I intend to find out!"

"Bess!" Wren stared at her in surprise. Bess usually wasn't curious about anything.

Bess crossed her arms. "I don't care what you say, Wren. "I'm going to find out who Tim's dad is. I want to know."

"So do I," said Paula. "We could work together and solve the mystery." Paula glanced at Wren and laughed.

Wren frowned. "What's so funny?"

"Bess and I are going to solve a mystery and you don't get to. So there!"

"Who cares? Besides, you don't know the first thing about solving a mystery. Your dad's a doctor, not a detective like mine."

"I'll have Bess to help me."

Wren shook her head. "What does Bess know?'

"I've learned a lot of things from you, Wren," said Bess. "I can use what I've learned to find out about Tim's dad."

"And then we'll tell everyone," said Paula. "It'll serve

Tim right! He's too poor to come to a private Christian school. He should go to the public school where he belongs."

Wren jabbed her hands into her jacket pockets so she wouldn't punch Paula. Paula was the one who didn't belong at Jordan Christian Academy. Up until this year Paula had gone to public school. Then her parents had decided to have her attend JCA, and Wren's life had been practically ruined. It was bad enough to have Paula as a neighbor, but to have her in the same school and in the same fifth grade was even worse.

"You leave Tim alone, Paula Gantz! I mean it!"

"You're not my boss, Wren House!" Paula turned to Bess. "Let's go to my house and we'll look in the phone book."

"Don't go with her, Bess! Please don't!" Wren caught at Bess's arm, but Bess pulled away. Bess rubbed her jacket sleeve smooth again. "This is important to me, Wren. This time I plan to solve a mystery. You're not the only curious girl, you know. Please, try to understand."

"Don't do this, Bess. You're the one who always wants to stay out of trouble and do what's right."

"Not this time! I'm tired of being your tagalong." Bess walked away with Paula and Paula shot a triumphant look at Wren.

Wren took a deep breath and forced back her anger. Jesus didn't want her to punch Paula or be angry with

Bess. "Help me, Lord," whispered Wren in an unsteady voice. "And help me to help Tim somehow."

Wren ran all the way to her house. She wanted to change from her school dress into jeans so she could ride her bike across town to Tim's house. She had to get to Tim and warn him to watch out for Paula and Bess before they made trouble for him.

2

THE LANDON BUILDING

After school, Tim leaned his ten-speed against the wide concrete steps of the Landon Building and slowly turned to Wren. His face was as gray as the sky and his blue eyes were sad. "Thanks for coming with me."

Wren shrugged. Just looking at him made her want to cry. "That's all right. I'm glad I could. I know you didn't want to come see Adam Landon."

"I hate to ask him for money! I hate him too! But Mom said I have to or she'll come herself. I can't let her do that." He shivered as he looked up at the grand building. "No, I couldn't let her come here."

Wren walked to the steps with Tim. She stopped with one foot on the bottom step. Two men walked around her and up to the wide glass doors. A cool wind ruffled her dark hair. "Why does Adam Landon give you money and gifts and things?"

Tim shrugged his thin shoulders. "I guess because he's rich and he likes me." He took a deep breath and stepped up one step, his jaw set with determination.

Wren slid her hand on the smooth railing that went up the middle of the steps. "How did you meet him?"

"In a Big Brother program. He was the leader and there wasn't anyone to be my Big Brother, so he did."

"I see." Wren slowed her pace to match Tim's. She felt small next to the adults walking up and down the steps. No one seemed to notice her or Tim and she was glad for that.

Suddenly, Tim stopped just outside the heavy glass doors that led into the huge office complex. "I can't do it! I can't ask him for money again!"

Wren saw the set look on his face and knew he meant what he said. "Why does she need money?"

"She says we're out of food, but we have as much as we usually do."

Wren knew that wasn't much at all. She knew Tim often ate a bowl of cereal for dinner as well as breakfast. His mother never fixed well-balanced meals the way her mom and dad did.

Tim trembled. "I think she wants it for . . . for . . . "

He couldn't finish, but Wren knew what he was going to say. Heather Avery always used any money she could get to buy bottles of wine or whiskey. Wren touched Tim's arm. "Since we're here, you could talk to Mr. Landon— just to talk to him. I'd like to meet him." Once she'd wished that he wouldn't help Tim, but now she was glad that he did. Tim needed a friend like Mr. Landon. "Maybe you should tell him that your dad lives right here in town. Maybe he'll help you find him."

Tim's jaw tightened and he shook his head.

"Why not?"

"If my dad really wanted to see me, he would. He knows where I live and he doesn't care about me at all! I hate him!"

"Oh, Tim! Don't say that! You know you can't hate anyone."

"Well, I do! I hate my dad and I always will!" Suddenly he pushed open the heavy door and stepped inside the warm carpeted lobby. A huge, live tree along with other shrubs stood near the center of the lobby. Water trickled down a stone wall to collect in a tiled pond where goldfish swam.

Wren looked up, up to the ceiling four stories high. She knew the Landon Building was full of plush offices. Dad had talked once about renting an office for himself, then decided to keep his office at home where he'd be close to the family and not have to pay the high rent each month. "Which floor is Mr. Landon's office on?"

"Top floor." Tim squared his thin shoulders and marched to the elevator with the glass sides. A woman walked out of one office and into another. "I hope he's not in."

"Didn't you call?"

"Yes, but he might not be in." Tim jabbed the up button.

"Didn't he say he would stay here until you came?"

"Yes."

"Then he'll be here." The elevator stopped with a smooth swish and the door slid open. Wren walked around Tim and stepped inside the elevator. "Hurry up, Tim, or the door will close."

Tim jumped in and pushed the button, then stood beside Wren and looked out the glass windows. He clenched and unclenched his fists. "I want to go home."

"You can later." Wren waited until the door slid open, then she stepped out and waited for Tim to join her. Green plants sat on the floor along the railing. The wide leaves looked as shiny as if someone had just cleaned and waxed them. Wren stopped and looked over the rail. "I'd hate to fall all the way down there." She shivered just thinking about it.

"Let's get out of here," whispered Tim.

"No, Tim. We're going to see Mr. Landon." Wren walked down the hall with an unwilling Tim beside her. They stopped at a large desk in a central reception area where a blonde woman sat. Tim knew she wasn't the receptionist or the secretary. He hadn't seen her before.

Frowning at them the woman said, "Children aren't allowed here without an adult."

Tim started to turn away, but Wren marched right up

16

to the desk. "We have an appointment with Adam Landon."

The woman narrowed her eyes, then reluctantly looked at the book on her desk. "Nothing is written here. Mr. Landon just stepped out and he didn't say when he'd be back. You two run along and play your game somewhere else."

Wren lifted her chin a fraction. "Tim does have an appointment!" Tim clutched at her jacket sleeve. "Let's go, Wren. It doesn't matter."

Wren reluctantly walked away from the desk with Tim. "I don't think we should leave," she whispered.

"I didn't want to come. Now I can tell Mom that Mr. Landon wasn't here."

Wren glanced over her shoulder just as the blonde woman disappeared through a door. Wren grabbed Tim's arm. "Quick! Where is Mr. Landon's office?"

"Over there." He pointed with a shaking finger.

"Let's go!" Wren tugged on Tim and they ran together to the office. Wren opened the door and they stepped inside to find the office empty.

"This is his secretary's office," said Tim. "That's his office." Tim pointed to a closed inner door.

Wren's legs trembled as she walked to the door and opened it. No one was inside and she relaxed slightly.

The room was large with a walnut desk, leather chair and sofa, a wall of shelves filled with books, and a tripod with a chalkboard on it. The walls were a rich wood paneling with pictures hanging on two walls. "This sure isn't like my dad's office! It's beautiful!"

"I like the office your dad has. It's ordinary and comfortable."

"I like it, too. When I'm a detective I think I'll have his kind of office instead of this." Wren touched the back of a leather chair. It smelled like a purse Mom carried. "I wonder where Mr. Landon is."

"Maybe he's inside the other office," said Tim as he walked to a closed door. "He goes in there when he meets with some of his clients." Tim turned the knob and eased open the door. He peeked inside.

"He's not there," he whispered. "A man that works for him is in there with another man."

Before he could pull the door shut, one of the men said, "I don't care what happens to Adam Landon! He can't have everything he wants, and that includes you."

"I don't know if I should go with you, Humphrey."

"Come on, Sid. Adam does good work and we both know it, but he's too honest. You need someone to handle your advertising who will play dirty once in a while. That's the only way to beat out your competitors."

Tim gripped Wren's arm and held a finger to his lips.

She nodded, understanding immediately.

Sid cleared his throat. "I suppose you're right, Humphrey, but I've dealt with Adam and with his father before him. I have a multimillion dollar furniture business and I don't want to lose it by going with you."

"You won't. You're going to go with me because you like the way I handle your ads. I'm the one who's been doing your campaign for almost five years now. Adam fired me today because I wasn't handling your ad campaign the way he wanted. He's too soft. The only way to beat out the competition is to tear them down and build yourself up. You agreed with my ad campaign for your sofas. I know you'll be happy if you go with me and leave the Landon Agency behind."

Wren stared in shock at Tim.

"Look, Humphrey, I have a contract with Adam."

"Easily handled. I'll steal the contract and you can say that it expired. I know Adam is out of his office for a few minutes. This would be a good time to get your contract."

Wren grabbed Tim and they ran to the door that led to the secretary's office.

"Follow my lead, Tim," she whispered. She stepped outside the door and into the secretary's office with Tim beside her. She eased the door closed. Perspiration popped out on her forehead and butterflies fluttered in her stomach. She waited until she heard men's voices, then she threw open the door. "Hey, Tim, is this Mr. Landon's office? Are you sure?"

"It's his office, all right. I've been here before. He said he'd meet me here."

Wren stopped short and stared at the two men as if she was totally shocked to see them. She memorized every detail about them so that she could describe them later. "You're not Adam Landon! We have an appointment with him!" She turned to Tim. "You said Mr. Landon would be here."

Tim nodded, following her lead just as she knew he would. He liked being a detective as much as she did. "He'll be here. He said he had time to talk with me." Tim looked at the men. "Did I meet you before when I was here?"

"No!" Humphrey glared at Tim. "I don't know how you got past Janice, but I want you both out of here right now!"

"We can't leave. Mr. Landon's expecting us." Wren scrambled onto the leather sofa and crossed her arms. Her legs stuck out straight in front of her. She put on her most stubborn look.

Tim leaned against the arm of the sofa. "I'm staying here, too. Mr. Landon always keeps his word and he said he'd meet me here."

"I'll talk with you later, Humphrey!"

"Wait, Sid! We'll get this settled!"

"You'd better!"

Humphrey glared at Tim and Wren, muttered under his breath, then turned away and followed Sid through the inner door.

Wren's dark eyes danced and she giggled behind her hand as he slammed the inner door behind them. Tim laughed under his breath.

3

DANGER

Tiptoeing to the door, Wren pressed her ear to it. "I don't hear anything," she whispered. "I think they're gone." She shivered. "I hope they're gone."

"Let's go then." Tim ran across the office, his tennis shoes silent on the thick, rust carpet.

"Wait!" Wren dashed around him and blocked his way. "We can't leave without telling Mr. Landon about Humphrey's terrible plan."

Tim shook his head stubbornly. "Mr. Landon wouldn't believe us."

"Why not?"

"We're only kids. Mr. Humphrey would say we were making it all up." Tim pushed past Wren. "I'm leaving right now. Are you coming?"

"No."

Tim stared at her, then walked out the door. It closed behind him with a click that rang inside Wren's head.

Wren looked around hesitantly. She hated being left

alone in a stranger's office. She really should follow Tim. She took a deep breath. Maybe she could leave a message for Mr. Landon. "I can't just leave without warning him."

She ran to his desk and tore off a sheet of paper from a memo pad. Grabbing a yellow pencil from beside the telephone, she thought for a minute, then wrote, "Mr. Landon, watch out for Humphrey. He's going to steal your client Sid and take his account away from you." She tapped the eraser against her chin and narrowed her eyes in thought. Finally she signed it, "A Friend." She tucked the note just under the edge of the memo pad and dropped the pencil beside it.

With a triumphant nod she dashed across the room. Maybe Tim had waited at the elevator for her, or even outside at their bikes. She turned the knob, but before she could open the door wide enough to walk through, she heard a woman's voice. Her heart zoomed to her feet. Had Janice caught Tim slipping from the office?

Wren eased the door open a little wider and peeked out just in time to see Heather Avery grab Tim and shake him hard. Wren gasped loud enough that Heather heard her.

Heather whirled around and Wren stepped slowly into the room. Heather tugged her jacket over her sweater. Her tangled red hair hung down on her shoulders. Her eyes were wild. Tim sank against the secretary's desk, his face white. Giant tears filled his eyes.

22

Heather shook her finger at Wren. "Don't you dare repeat what you overheard! It's not your business!" She spun around to face Tim. "Now, get that money from Adam and get it today!"

Tim only stared at her, not speaking and not moving.

Wren swallowed hard. What had Heather Avery said to Tim? With an unsteady hand Wren tucked her dark hair behind her ears. Maybe she should call for help. Heather Avery looked very angry. Before Wren could do anything, Heather jerked open the door and walked out into the hallway, closing the door with a firm snap.

Tim sank to the floor with his back against the desk, his knees pulled up to his chin, and his arms around his skinny legs. He shivered, but still didn't speak.

Wren dropped beside him and looked into his ashen face. Her heart beat faster. "What did she say to you?"

Tim didn't move.

"What's wrong, Tim?"

He swallowed hard.

"Tim, you're scaring me!"

He shivered again. "I . . . let's get . . . let's go."

"Tim, what's wrong? Did she beat you?" Wren looked for bruises, but didn't find any, "Tim?"

He licked his lips. "My . . . dad."

Wren frowned. "Your dad?"

"She . . . told me."

"Oh, Tim!" Wren leaned close enough that she could

smell Tim's skin. "She told you who he is?"

Tim nodded slightly. A tear slipped from his eye and ran down his cheek on a path of freckles.

Wren jumped up and looked down at Tim. "Well?"

Slowly, unsteadily he pushed himself up.

"Tim? Who is it?"

Tim leaned weakly against the desk.

"Do I know him?" She wanted to shake the secret from him, but she kept her hands locked together in front of her.

With his head down, Tim walked to the door. "I'm leaving," he said just above a whisper.

"What about Mr. Landon?"

"What about him?"

"He's your friend. You don't want Humphrey to cheat him, do you?"

Tim shuddered. "I'm leaving. You do what you want." But he clung to the door as if he'd fall if he let go.

Wren ran to his side and touched his arm. "Tim, tell me what your mother said."

"So you can laugh at me?"

"Would I laugh?"

He lifted his face and his angry blue eyes clashed with her brown ones. "Why don't you use your great power of deductive reasoning to figure it out?"

She fell back a step with her hand at her throat. "Are you mad at me?"

"I'm mad at everybody!" His voice broke and he cleared his throat. "I hate my mom and my dad and right now I even hate you, Wren House!"

The color drained from Wren's face and she dropped her hand to her side. Even when she'd hated him, he hadn't hated her.

Tim stumbled out the door and ran to the elevator.

Wren took an unsteady step to follow him, then stopped in alarm. Humphrey, with her note to Mr. Landon in his hand, and the man Sid walked out of a door to her right, talking earnestly. Wren held her breath. If they looked toward the elevator they'd see Tim. If they turned her way, they'd see her. Her mouth turned bone dry. Her legs felt too weak to hold her slight weight. She bit her lip to keep from crying out to Tim. She stood very still to keep the men from catching a glimpse of movement.

What would happen if Tim turned and called to her? She trembled.

Just then the doors of the elevator slid open. Tim stepped part way in, then turned to look back at Wren. He saw the men just as they turned and spotted him.

"Hey, kid!" shouted Humphrey.

Wren sped across to the elevator, pushing Tim all the way inside. He fell against the bar and clung to it. She pushed the button and the door closed, almost catching Humphrey's hand. Wren saw the anger on the man's face as he turned to say something to the other man, then they both turned and ran.

"They're heading for the stairs!" cried Wren. She jabbed the buttom to go up again to the same floor. "We can't let them catch us, Tim."

Tim stood up, squared his shoulders, shook himself as if to wake up, and stepped beside Wren. "We'll have to think of a plan. We can't let them catch us." His voice was almost back to normal.

"I think we should go back to Mr. Landon's office and wait for him."

Tim shook his head and backed away. "No, no. I won't go back there. I won't"

"But why?"

Tim plucked at the sleeve of his jacket. "Don't ask." He sounded as if he would burst into tears.

Just then the door slid open. Wren grabbed Tim's arm, dragging him out of the elevator. Down the hall, Janice sat at her desk. She stood up when she saw them and shook her head. Wren ignored her and pulled Tim to Mr. Landon's office. She opened the door and pushed Tim inside.

"Let me out of here, Wren! I will not stay in here! I mean it!" Tim shoved against Wren to push her aside but she wouldn't move.

"Stop it, Tim! We have to talk to Mr. Landon and get his help."

Tim shook his head.

"You're being dumb, Tim. Why don't you want to talk to him?"

"Because he's my dad!" The words rang out and hung in the air between them.

Wren's mouth dropped open. "What?"

"You heard me."

She gulped and shook her head. "I can't believe it."

"It's true," Tim said grimly.

"How do you know?"

He shuddered. "Mom told me a few minutes ago. We were fighting about asking him for money and she said he has to give us money any time we ask. I asked why and she . . . she told me."

"Oh, Tim!"

Tim doubled his fists and a muscle jumped in his jaw. "I never want to see Adam Landon again as long as I live."

"Does he know . . . he's your . . . dad?"

"Yes."

"Oh, Tim." She had so much she wanted to say, but no words came.

"Let's get out of here."

She nodded, then shook her head. "But we can't. Those men are after us and they don't want us to make trouble. We have to ask Mr. Landon to keep us safe."

"I won't ask him for anything!" The freckles stood out boldly on his pale face.

"We have to do something, Tim. We're in danger."

"We'll go talk to your dad and let him take care of it. Or your mom. She's a lawyer and she'll know what to do, but I will not talk to Adam Landon. I will never talk to him again as long as I live."

Just then the knob turned and Wren froze, her eyes glued to the opening door.

4

FACE TO FACE

Tim moved closer to Wren as the door opened wide. A well dressed man in his late twenties or early thirties stepped inside. He had reddish-brown hair, cut and combed neatly, blue eyes that seemed to see everything, and he stood almost six feet tall. Wren thought he was very good looking, almost as handsome as her dad.

"Tim!" The man stepped forward with a warm smile and a hand out.

Tim didn't move, nor speak. Finally Mr. Landon dropped his hand.

Wren looked from one to the other. She saw a puzzled look cross Mr. Landon's face when Tim kept silent. She took a deep breath. "Hi. I'm Wren, Tim's friend. We came to see you."

Mr. Landon looked down at Wren. He smiled slightly. "I'm glad to meet you, Wren." He turned back to Tim with a dark brow lifted. "I've been looking for you. You said you had to see me." He was quiet, giving Tim a chance to speak, but Tim remained silent. "What can I do for you?"

Tim's eyes darkened with fresh anger. "Nothing! Not a thing—now or ever!"

"What?" Impatiently Mr. Landon flipped back his jacket and stood with his hands on his hips. "What's gotten into you, Tim?"

"As if you don't know!"

"Well, I don't know!" He leaned down toward Tim. "You called me and asked me if you could come see me. Now you're suddenly acting hostile."

"I . . . I hate you!" Tim turned and ran from the room.

Mr. Landon frowned at the closed door. "That's strange. What's wrong with him?"

Wren could have told him, but she only shrugged.

"Aren't you going with him?"

"Yes, but first I have to warn you." Her stomach tightened.

She rubbed her damp palms down her jacket. "Tim and I were in your office a while ago and we overhead two men plotting against you."

Mr. Landon chuckled. "Plotting? Have you been watching too much TV?"

"No. I'm serious. My dad is Sam House, the famous private detective. He's taught me a lot about the business."

"Is that so?"

"Yes. I know what I'm talking about. I can smell trouble

before it strikes."

Mr. Landon laughed. "You don't say."

Wren frowned and squirmed uncomfortably. Tim should've stayed to help her. "We, Tim and I, overheard two men talking." Suddenly she felt too hot in the room. She unzipped her jacket. "One was a man who works for you named Humphrey and the other man was a client of yours called Sid. Humphrey plans to steal your client, Sid."

Adam Landon cracked his knuckles. "I don't like this game you're playing. It's not funny. Tim was smart to run away."

The color drained from Wren's face. Mr. Landon didn't believe her! How could she convince him differently? "Do you have a man named Humphrey working for you?"

"Geoff Humphrey. He's my vice president."

"And you fired him."

"Why do you think that?" He rattled the keys in his pockets.

"I heard him say so."

Mr. Landon fingered his tie. "Strange."

"Strange?"

He nodded. "I haven't done it yet, but I've been planning to."

"Maybe he knew it and he wants to get back at you. We did hear him say that he was going to take Sid from you."

Mr. Landon strode across the room and back to stop

before Wren. His face was dark with anger. "I don't know what game you're playing, little girl, but I think you should leave right now. This isn't funny."

Wren's lip quivered. "I'm telling the truth. Call my dad to verify that I'm a truthful person." Even feeling as badly as she did, she liked the feel of the word verify on her lips. She'd heard Dad and Mom use it often. "Call my mother. She's probably still in her office. It's just a block from here."

"And who is your mother?"

"Lorrene House. She's a lawyer with Brownlee and Towns."

"They're my lawyers."

"Then you know my mom."

"No, I don't know her. I work only with Chester Brownlee."

"Well, she knows you. I guess everyone knows you."

"I don't know about that."

She studied him thoughtfully. Did he know that Tim knew he was his father? Maybe she should tell him.

Mr. Landon clamped a well manicured hand on Wren's thin shoulder. "I think this conversation is finished. You go home and don't bother me again with your little game. Tell Tim that I'm disappointed in him."

Wren pulled away and stood at her fullest height. Beside him she was tiny and short, a mere child. "I wish you would believe that Tim and I did hear Humphrey plotting against you."

"Then why didn't Tim stay and tell me himself?"

"Because he couldn't face you."

He looked at her suspiciously. "Why not?"

Wren twisted her toe in the carpet. Desperately she wanted to tell him, but she knew Tim wouldn't like it. "I can't say."

"Can't?"

She swallowed hard. "Won't. Tim should tell you himself."

"Why did he run out of here so fast?"

Wren shrugged. A shiver ran down her spine.

"Why was he here?"

"His mother said he should get some money from you." Wren's voice cracked and she flushed painfully.

His eyes narrowed. "She did, did she?"

Wren nodded.

"Just how much did she want?"

"I don't know."

He reached in his pocket, pulled out a twenty dollar bill and held it out to her. "This is all I have on me. Take it to Heather. Tell her . . . Never mind. You'd better give the money to Tim so that he can buy some groceries with it."

Wren hesitated, then took it just to keep Tim out of more trouble with his mother. She pushed it into her jeans pocket. "I'll make sure they get it. Thank you." She looked at him helplessly. "Please, please take my word on

Humphrey."

"Why?"

"For Tim's sake?"

"Why for Tim's sake?"

"I'm his friend, and he'd be really mad at you if you didn't trust me."

He rubbed his cheek thoughtfully. "I'll check into it."

"If you need me to investigate further, I will." She waited for his answer.

His face was very somber, but she saw a twinkle in his eye. "I'll keep that in mind. Thank you."

"It was nice meeting you, Mr. Landon." She held out her hand and he shook it, releasing it with a low laugh. "I'll give Tim the money. He'll probably call you to thank you."

"It doesn't matter."

Wren hesitated. "Maybe you should go see Tim."

"Any reason?"

"Yes."

He narrowed his eyes. "What is it?"

"I can't . . . I can't tell you." Wren snapped her mouth closed before she did tell him, then walked away with a quick goodbye.

Wren peeked around the hall for any sign of Humphrey, but didn't see him. She slipped inside the elevator and rode it down. Several people stood on each landing, but no one rang for the elevator so it didn't stop until the

34

ground floor. Finally outdoors she breathed easier. The cool breeze felt good on her face. She walked to her bike and wheeled it to the sidewalk. Neither Tim nor his bike were in sight.

"Hey, you, little girl!"

She glanced up to see Humphrey just a few feet away. A shiver ran down her back. In a flash she leaped on her bike and pedaled away at top speed. She didn't stop until she reached Tim's yard. She dropped her bike beside his and ran to the door. Her chest rose and fell as perspiration dampened her face and neck. She lifted her dark hair off the back of her neck to cool it, took a deep breath and knocked on the door.

Tim answered immediately. "What're you doing here?" He pushed on the door, but she stuck out her hand and stopped it.

"I have money from Mr. Landon."

"I don't want it."

"I brought it so your mom wouldn't be mad at you." She pulled it from her jeans and held it out.He hesitated, then grabbed it and stuck it in his shirt pocket.

"And Humphrey chased me."

"What?" Tim shot out the door. "Did he hurt you?"

"No." She shivered. "But he scared me.

"Tim's eyes widened. "Tell me everything!"

"About Mr. Landon?"

"No!"

"You have to talk to him sometime, Tim."

Tim turned his back to the wind and looked up at the gray sky. "You'd better go home before it rains."

Wren shook her head. "It's not going to rain, Tim. And I don't have to be home yet. It's Neil's turn to help in the kitchen."

"Well, you can stay if you don't try to talk about Adam Landon."

She sighed heavily. "He wouldn't believe me when I told him about Humphrey stealing his client, Sid. Humphrey tried to talk to me outside the building, but I got out of there fast."

"I'm glad."

"But Mr. Landon didn't believe me!"

"You tried, Wren. That's all you can do."

"You could try, Tim. He'd believe you."

Tim's face hardened. "I won't talk to him. I mean it, Wren, so don't try anything."

Wren twisted a strand of dark hair around her finger. "Tim, you know you must forgive your mom and your . . . dad for not telling you the truth."

Tim doubled his fists. "I'll never forgive them!"

A giant tear welled up in Wren's eye and she turned her face away before Tim saw it.

5

A TALK WITH AMOS PIKE

Wren looked back at Tim from under her long lashes. His face was still set stubbornly and she knew she couldn't say another word to him about Adam Landon. She cleared her throat. "Have you seen Amos Pike lately?"

Tim watched a car drive past. "Two days ago."

"Me, too. How about going to see him now before I have to go home."

"Sure. All right." Tim touched his pocket with the twenty dollar bill in it. "Maybe I should give this to Mom first."

"No!" Wren shook her head. "Mr. Landon said that you should buy groceries with it yourself instead of giving it all to your mom."

Tim's face turned brick red. "He knows what she'd do with it and still he gives it to her! He makes me so mad!"

"You don't hate him, Tim. You're angry with him, but you don't hate him. You know God gave you a spirit of love and not hate."

Tim glared at Wren with his fists doubled at his sides. "Will you be quiet? I hate him and I always will!"

With a heavy sigh Wren turned away and lifted her bike. Silently she prayed for Tim and for his mother and even for his dad.

"Are you mad at me, Wren?"

"No."

"Do you still want to visit Amos?"

"Yes."

She followed Tim across Bond and over to Green Street. The clouds parted and a weak sun shone. The wind blew colored leaves from the oaks and maples and sent them spiraling to the lawns and streets and on top of parked cars.

They found Amos in his front yard looking at the last of the tiny marigolds along the edge of his cracked sidewalk. He smiled from ear to ear when he saw Tim and Wren.

"Hi, kids," he said. He was dressed in worn jeans, black engineer boots and a denim jacket with frayed cuffs. A blue cap sat on his balding head. His little black dog, Buster, ran to them with a happy bark.

Tim bent down to Buster and pulled him close.

Amos crossed his arms. "What's new with you two?"

"Nothing," said Tim.

"Everything!" said Wren even before Tim's answer was finished.

Amos pulled off his cap, rubbed his thin gray hair and settled his cap back in place. "I think something's up with you two. Want to tell me?"

"Tim does," said Wren.

"I do not!"

"So, it's that way, is it?" Amos clamped a wrinkled hand on Tim's shoulder. A look of love softened his lined face. "You helped me when I needed it. How about giving me a chance to help you?"

"Please do, Tim. Please." Wren stepped right in front of Tim and pleaded silently with him.

Tim looked at her for a long time, glanced up at Amos, then dropped his chin to his chest. "All right! I'll tell you, Amos. But it won't do any good."

"We'll see about that. Let's go inside and talk." Amos led the way into his small house, took their jackets and motioned for them to sit on the couch. The warm room was in perfect order even though it was shabby. A green ivy plant hung at the window. Magazines lay in a pile on the coffee table. A green, black and red afghan that Mrs. Pike had crocheted just before she'd died hung on the back of the couch. The aroma of coffee filled the air.

Wren settled into the corner of the couch so that she could watch Tim as well as Amos who sat in the soft chair across from the couch. Buster settled at Amos's feet. Wren liked visiting with Amos. He always had time for them. She was glad they'd become friends after solving the mystery at the Wheeler place.

"What's happened to make your eyes look so sad, Tim?" asked Amos in a gentle voice.

Tim rubbed the back of his hand across his nose.

"Tell it all," said Wren.

Tim shot her a warning look so she snapped her mouth closed and crossed her arms over her thin chest.

Amos leaned forward and narrowed his eyes. "Is your mother worse?"

"My mother? Worse? No, my mother's not worse. She's just the same." Tim's voice broke. He knotted his hands into fists, then opened them to press his hands against his thin legs. "Always the same. Always drunk. Always after more money to buy more to drink."

"You sound very angry," said Amos.

"Shouldn't I be? Who wants a drunk for a mother? I sure don't! I hate her!"

"Tim!" cried Wren. She'd never heard him say such terrible things even when his mother embarrassed or hurt him.

"I can tell you're badly hurt," said Amos. He reached over and patted Tim's jeans-clad leg. "Tell me what happened."

Tim shuddered. He picked up a small red throw pillow that clashed with his hair and freckles and hugged it to him. "I found out today that my dad is . . . is Adam Landon."

"I thought as much."

Wren gasped and Tim leaped to his feet. Buster lifted his head and barked.

"You knew?" cried Tim.

"I've heard gossip, and I put two and two together."

"What two and two?" asked Wren. It really was embarrassing to think that as a great detective with a sharp mind she hadn't even suspected that Adam Landon was more than a friend to Tim.

Amos shook his head and help up his hand. "Never mind. Sit down, Tim, and tell me the rest."

Tim sank to the edge of the couch with his hands locked on his knees. "What more could there be? I think it's terrible that all these years Mom knew and Adam knew and maybe the whole world knew but they didn't tell me."

"They should've told you," said Amos. "But they didn't. So, you have to go on from there."

"I hate them both!"

"But you can't, Tim!" cried Wren. "You know God doesn't want you to hate anyone!"

"That's right," said Amos. "When you let hatred and unforgiveness stay inside you, it blocks out your communication with God. Remember how I hated my sister, Stella? It almost ruined my happiness. We forgave each other with God's help. Now we're happy. God wants the very best for you, but He can't give it to you if you allow Satan to make you hate."

Tim ducked his head and muttered, "I know."

"Then forgive your mom and your dad. Let go of the hate you feel right now."

"But I can't!"

"With God's help, you can." Amos nodded and smiled encouragingly at Tim.

"We'll pray with you," whispered Wren.

"If you want."Tim sat quietly for a long time, then finally nodded.

Amos moved over to sit between them on the couch and put an arm around each. He prayed for Tim and then Wren prayed, and finally Tim did.

"I'm glad you want to be like Jesus," said Wren.

Tim smiled weakly at Wren. "Me, too. I'm sorry for being mean to you."

"That's okay. I forgive you."

Amos hugged them both and Buster barked as if he knew just what was happening.

"Now, we can help Mr. Landon," said Wren.

"Why does he need help?" asked Amos.

"You tell him." said Tim.

Wren quickly told the story, and Amos whistled softly in surprise. "I tried to tell Mr. Landon, but he didn't believe me."

"That's only because he doesn't know you," said Amos.

Wren smiled and pressed her cheek against Amos's arm. "Thanks."

"I don't think he'll believe me, either," said Tim.

"First you tell him that you know he's your dad," said Amos. "I think he'll be glad that you know. After that, he might have more of an open mind to listen to your story."

Tim rubbed his hands down his jeans. "What if he doesn't want me to know that I'm his . . . his son?"

"Then he'll have to deal with it. Honesty is the best policy." Amos ruffled Tim's hair. "Once he knows that you know, maybe he'll want to be a bigger part of your life. He might even be able to help your mother stop drinking."

"If that's possible," muttered Tim.

"I saw a program on TV about a hospital where alcoholics stay until they can stop drinking. Maybe your mother could go there."

"She wouldn't," said Tim just above a whisper. "I already talked to her about it."

"I think we should all pray for your mother every day," said Amos. "We have God on our side and He wants the very best for your mother just as He does for us."

Tim smiled up at Amos Pike, his eyes thanking him.

"You kids tell me if there's anything more that I can do to help," said Amos as he handed them their jackets a few minutes later.

"We will," said Wren. "Maybe you should call Mr. Landon and tell him that I'm a truthful person and a good detective."

"If it'd help, I would, but he doesn't know me from

Buster here." Amos chuckled and Buster wriggled all over.

Several minutes later Tim and Wren stopped at the corner grocery to buy a few groceries. Tim sighed heavily as he pushed the cart down the aisle.

"Mom's going to be mad when she finds out I used the money for groceries. Maybe I should spend only ten dollars and give her the rest."

Just then Bess and Paula walked around the end of the aisle and spotted Wren and Tim. Bess turned away with a red face, but Paula marched right up to them.

"We looked in the phone book for Avery," snapped Paula, glaring right at Tim as if it was his fault that she'd failed. "I want to know about your dad and I want to know right now."

The color drained from Tim's face, and he looked helplessly at Wren.

"It's none of your business, Paula." Wren pushed the cart forward. "I'm helping Tim buy groceries and then I have to go home." She looked straight at Bess. "I can't believe you, Bess. Why are you being so nosy?"

Bess walked up to Wren. "Why is it called nosy when I'm doing it and detective work when you're doing it?"

Wren's brain whirled for an answer, but she had none. With a flip of her dark hair she turned to Tim. "Let's finish and get out of here."

"We'll find out the truth yet," Paula called after them.

Tim stopped beside the apples and turned to Wren,

his eyes wide with fear. "Do you think they'll find out?"

Wren bit her bottom lip. Paula usually learned what she wanted to and with Bess helping, it was possible. "We'd better get your groceries, Tim." She didn't have the heart to tell him what she thought.

They finished quickly. Just as Tim picked up a bag of apples, Wren glanced back to find Bess and Paula following them. "Are you girls hungry? Want a Cheerio?"

Bess shook her head and Paula lifted her chin and wrinkled her nose in disgust.

"I guess they're not hungry," said Wren.

Her stomach tightened, though, as the two girls walked away. Was it possible that Bess and Paula were going to become best friends? Wren swallowed hard as she waited for the clerk to ring up the groceries. Maybe she should forget about helping Tim and see if Bess wanted to talk about Neil and Brian.

"It's too late to see Adam today," said Tim, breaking into her thoughts. "Shall we go right after school tomorrow?"

"We only have half a day tomorrow. That would be a good day to go." Wren glanced around at Bess and saw her leaving with Paula. She wanted to grab her words back. Maybe she would lose Bess's friendship totally if she spent the day with Tim.

An icy band tightened around her heart as she walked out of the store with Tim.

6

TROUBLE

Friday morning Wren ran down the sidewalk, her school bag swinging from her hand. Her skirt swished against her legs. Tiny puddles stood on the sidewalk from last night's rain. Up ahead of her, the bright sun shining on Bess's hair turned it even lighter. "Wait for me, Bess!"

Bess turned and quickly brushed away a tear.

Wren ran to her side. "What's wrong?"

"What do you care?" For once Bess's blonde hair had a few strands out of place. The collar of her blue blouse was half in and half out of her jacket.

Wren looked at Bess with a puzzled frown. "What do you mean? You know I care. We're best friends."

"We are? I needed to talk to you, but you were always gone! I thought you and Tim were best friends the way you're always hanging around him."

"I'm not <u>always</u> with him!"

"You have been the last few days." Bess sniffed and wiped away another tear. She walked slowly and Wren fell into step beside her.

Wren peeked sideways at Bess. "Why're you crying?"

"If you weren't so busy with Tim, you'd know."

"Know what?"

Bess looked around to make sure no one could hear her. She leaned close to Wren. "Neil. That's what!"

"Neil? What's my brother done now?" Wren had two brothers; Neil was in the eighth grade and Philip in the eleventh grade. Girls always envied her because she lived with them, but she couldn't understand what was so great about it.

Bess looked horrified. "Don't you know?"

Wren shook her head. "I saw him at dinner last night and this morning for breakfast. He looked all right. He said he was having a little trouble with his computer."

Bess clutched her book bag and great tears filled her blue eyes. "Wren, Neil walked to school twice with Carin Johns! You know Carin Johns. She's gorgeous! And smart. And she's in the eighth grade with Neil!"

"Maybe they were working on a school project together."

"I don't believe that for a minute." Bess dashed away her tears and walked several steps without speaking. "I think he's in love with her."

"Not Neil. He doesn't like girls yet. Philip does, but not Neil."

"How do you know? You never notice anything but Tim Avery!"

"That's not true! I have the keen eye of a detective."

"Then why didn't you see Neil with Carin?"

Wren ducked her head and watched the cracks in the sidewalk as they walked. "I guess I just didn't notice. There are some things I don't see, you know."

"Even if it had been Brian Davies with Carin, you still wouldn't have noticed!"

Wren shot a look around to make sure no one had heard Bess's outburst. She didn't want anyone to know that she liked Brian Davies.

"Don't say his name right out here where people can hear."

"I just might tell Paula Gantz that you're in love with Brian."

Wren grabbed Bess's arm. "Don't you dare tell Paula! I mean it!"

"Maybe I already told her."

Wren gasped. If Paula knew, she'd tell everyone, especially Brian.

"Did you?"

Bess shook her head. "No. I didn't tell."

Wren breathed easier. "That's a relief!"

Bess walked around a tricycle. "Has Neil said anything about liking Carin?"

Wren walked in silence as she thought of everything that Neil had said. "I heard him talk about his computer and his school science project and that's all."

"Did you listen carefully?"

Wren rolled her eyes. "Who can listen to everything the boys talk about?"

"I could."

"You probably could. But they don't listen to me talk about my detective work. They think I'm too young to be a real detective."

"That's why you like Tim, isn't it? He listens to you and he wants to be a detective just like you when he grows up."

Wren nodded. "That's why I like him. He can spot a mystery as quickly as I can."

Bess stuck out her bottom lip in a pout. "I know you like Tim better than me."

"I do not!"

"Yes, you do or you'd help me with Neil. We haven't talked about Neil and Brian for a long, long time."

"We haven't had time."

Bess pointed an unsteady finger at Wren. "You haven't had time!"

Wren's stomach tightened. Bess was right. Somehow she'd been so occupied with other things that she hadn't had time for Bess. "We could today."

Bess turned to Wren with a smile and sparkling eyes. "We only have half a day of school today. We could spend the whole afternoon talking about them."

Wren's heart dropped. She'd forgotten about her plans with Tim. She took a deep breath and let it out slowly. "I'm sorry, Bess. But I can't."

"You can't?"

"Sorry. Tim and I have something important to do today."

"Tim? You?" Bess stamped her foot. "I might've known!"

"You and I can play tomorrow. All day since it's Saturday." Wren smiled stiffly. "We could, Bess."

"Oh, sure, just like we can this afternoon." Bess faced Wren. "I don't want to be best friends with you any longer. I'm going to play with Paula. So there!"

"Don't, Bess. Please."

"I'm going to do what Paula wants and I'm going to go with her to find out who Tim's dad is. And when we find out, we're going to tell everyone in the whole world!"

"No! You can't Bess. You know you shouldn't."

"Watch me! Do you know who Tim's dad is?"

A shiver ran down Wren's spine. She dare not slip and tell Bess the name of Tim's dad. "What if I do?"

Bess peered closely at Wren. "Do you, Wren?"

Wren lifted her chin and clamped her mouth closed.

"I know that look, Wren. You know, but you won't tell."

"I didn't say that."

"So, who cares if you know? I'm going to find out and I'm going to tell everyone. Bess held her book bag close to her and raced the rest of the way to the school.

"Bess, you don't know what trouble you're making,"

Wren whispered.

Slowly she trudged on alone until she was on the sidewalk just outside the school. She saw Tim lock his bike in place. He looked up and spotted her, waved and ran to her side.

"Hi, Wren. What's wrong?"

Wren shifted her book bag from one hand to another. "Bess and I just had a fight."

"I'm sorry."

"Me, too." She walked slowly up the walk. At the front door of the school, boys and girls stood waiting for the first bell, talking and laughing.

Tim touched her arm and stopped her. "I gave Mom some of the money yesterday. She hugged me." Tim blushed. "She was glad I bought groceries. She even fixed supper last night."

"That's great!" Wren knew how unusual it was.

"I think she was sorry she told me about . . . about Adam."

"Did you call him last night?"

Tim shook his head. "I thought about it, but I just couldn't."

"Well, we'll see him today. Maybe we won't have any trouble convincing him that Humphrey is out to steal his client. He might already believe that I told him the truth yesterday."

A movement behind Wren caught her attention and

she spun around to find Paula sneaking up on them to eavesdrop. Wren shook her finger at Paula. "Stop spying! Mind your own business for once."

Paula flipped back her hair. "I'm making you and Tim my business. I'm going to find out everything!"

"Leave me alone," snapped Tim.

"I am going to learn the truth, Tim Avery. You might as well tell me now." Paula looked very sure of herself.

"Leave him alone," said Wren. Tim turned and ran to the crowd of boys from fifth grade.

Paula laughed a short, loud laugh. "I'm going to find out who his dad is before you do, Bird House."

"You're too late! I already know!" Wren was sorry the second the words were out. Paula had wanted to trick her into admitting that she knew and she'd fallen into the trap. Anger rushed through Wren. She wanted to stamp her foot in the puddle nearby and splash dirty water all over Paula's skirt.

Paula laughed loud and long. "You're not as smart as you think you are, Bird House. I'm much smarter than you. And I'm more popular and prettier."

Wren's hand tingled with the desire to slap Paula. But she couldn't. She knew Jesus didn't want her to. "You think what you want, Paula."

Wren marched away with her head high.

Just then someone ran through a puddle and splashed dirty water on her bare legs.

"Watch it!" she cried. She turned her head to find Brian Davies beside her. She wanted the sidewalk to open up and swallow her.

Brian smiled. "Sorry, Wren. I didn't notice the puddle."

Her heart stopped, then raced on and her face turned bright red. She just stood there with her mouth open and no words coming out.

"See you later." Brian dashed off and she could breathe again.

In a daze Wren looked around for Bess. Wren finally spotted her deep in conversation with Paula Gantz. Wren just sighed heavily and turned away. How could she survive if she couldn't tell Bess about her grand experience with Brian Davies?

Just then the bell rang. Wren followed the others into school, her heart fluttering as she relived the moment with Brian.

7

DETECTIVE WORK

Just outside Wren's back door Tim touched her arm to stop her. He looked worried. "Are you sure it's all right if I eat lunch with you?"

"Of course it's all right. We have a rule at our house."

"What rule?"

"We can invite friends to lunch as long as we help clean up after."

Tim puffed out his chest. "I don't mind helping."

He always helped when he ate with them. He never remembered that he was welcome for a meal. At his house no one was ever welcome, not for a meal and not for a visit.

As Tim walked in ahead of her, Wren glanced over her shoulder, then frowned. She saw Bess and Paula duck quickly behind a bush.

"I can't believe it!" Wren dashed across the yard to the bush and stood before them with her hands on her hips. "What do you want?"

Paula lifted her chin. "We're spying on you, that's what."

Wren gasped. She glanced toward the house where Tim waited outside the door. "Why would you spy on me?"

Bess narrowed her blue eyes. "Because of Tim. We're going to shadow you all day long. Surveillance is what you call it, isn't it?"

"Don't do this, Bess." Wren looked at her friend with wide, begging eyes. She'd tried over and over all morning to talk to Bess to tell her about Brian Davies, but Bess had refused to talk. "Please, leave Tim alone. You don't know what you're doing."

Bess turned away, but not before Wren caught the glimmer of tears in her eyes.

Paula stepped right up to Wren. "We'll leave Tim alone as soon as we learn the truth and not before!" She turned to Bess. "Let's go to my house and watch from there."

Wren pressed her lips together and watched them run across the street to Paula's house. Somehow she and Tim would have to sneak away to keep the girls from following them.

Tim called, "What's wrong, Wren?"

She ran to him. "Oh, Bess and Paula think they're going to follow us all day until they learn the truth. But we're too smart for them."

"I wish they'd leave me alone!"

"I do, too. Maybe we should tell Bess the truth about

your dad. Without her help Paula wouldn't get anywhere."

Tim's eyes widened in shock. "No way! I don't want anyone to know!"

"All right." Wren flung out her arms. "Forget it and let's go eat."

An hour later Wren stopped halfway up the steps to the glass doors of the Landon Building and frowned at Tim. She and Tim had had grilled cheese sandwiches, milk, and apples for dessert at her house with Neil and Dad. Philip had gone to a friend's house and Mom hadn't been able to get home for lunch. Afterward, they'd sneaked out the back way, being careful that they weren't followed by Bess and Paula.

"You should've tried to call him again, Tim. Maybe he was out to lunch."

"I didn't want to talk to him, Wren."

"All right. But if he's not there, we'll leave another note. And we won't leave it where Humphrey can take it." Her ears burned. Would she ever be as smart as Dad? She walked to the door of the big building and pushed it open.

Tim followed her in and stopped near the tree, his face white. "Wren, I can't see him! I can't tell him that I know he's my dad!" His voice was low and strained. He looked as if he might run away any second.

"Sure you can, Tim. I'll help you." She tugged him toward the elevator. They could see it on the fourth floor. She pushed the down button and watched it slip down the tracks. A woman and two men were inside. Wren could see that they were talking and laughing. The door slip open and laughter spilled out. The woman and men walked out and Wren and Tim stepped into the elevator. Wren pushed the up button. The door closed and the elevator started up smoothly.

Just then Wren saw the outer doors open and Bess and Paula enter. "I can't believe it!" Anger rushed through her. She saw Bess glance around and Paula look toward the elevator. Wren tried to move out of sight, but there was no way.

"What's wrong?" asked Tim.

"They found us!" Wren pointed and Tim peered down just as Paula pointed up for Bess to see them.

"They make me so mad! How could they know where we were?" Tim jammed his hands into his pockets and turned so that he couldn't see the girls.

"I don't know! They make me mad, too."

The door slid open and Wren jumped out with Tim on her heels. They ran toward Adam Landon's office, but before they reached it Janice spotted them.

"Stop right there, you two!" Janice ran down the hall toward them. Her blonde hair streamed out behind her. Her face was grim, and she looked nine feet tall.

"Let's go!" cried Wren. She sped toward Adam Landon's office door, her heart thudding painfully against her ribcage.

"Wren!"

She turned at Tim's frantic cry to find that Janice held him in a firm grip. She shot a look toward the door, then back at Tim. Should she get Mr. Landon to help her or should she find a way to set Tim free?

Before she could do anything the elevator door slid open and Bess and Paula stepped out. Bess froze when she saw Wren, but Paula laughed and strode forward as if she belonged in the Landon Building.

"More kids!" cried Janice, dropping her hands to glare at the new arrivals. "I want all of you out of here this instant."

"We have business here," said Paula. "My dad is a doctor and he sent me here with a message for . . ."

"For Mr. Landon!" cried Wren.

Paula nodded. "Yes, for Mr. Landon. If we don't get to see him right now, my dad will be really angry."

"Mr. Landon isn't here and he won't be back for several minutes."

"We'll wait," said Paula. With her head high she walked forward. She headed in the wrong direction but Wren grabbed her arm and headed her in the right direction.

Tim opened the door to the Landon Agency and let the girls enter first. He walked in after them and closed the door before Janice could step inside.

Gina Tebra looked up from her typing, "What's this?"

"Hi, Mrs. Tebra," said Tim, his face red.

"Hello, Tim." Gina pushed her long black hair over her slender shoulder. Her dark eyes were kind as she studied Tim. "Do you have an appointment with Mr. Landon today?"

Tim moved restlessly. He looked out of place in the plush office with his worn jeans and dirty tennis shoes. "I have to see him, Mrs. Tebra."

"He stepped out and won't be back for awhile."

"We'll wait," said Wren. She turned to Bess and Paula. "Thanks for helping us, but now we can manage on our own."

"Why do you want to see Adam Landon?" asked Paula suspiciously.

"Does he know . . . you know?" Bess stepped closer to Wren.

Wren knew that Bess wanted to find out if Adam Landon knew who Tim's dad was. Wren fingered the cuff of her sweater.

"He might. Tim has to talk to him to see."

"I'm waiting right here," said Paula. She dropped on the couch and crossed her arms.

"So am I," said Bess, dropping beside Paula. Wren looked helplessly from the girls to Tim. Finally she sat down, too. "Tim, we'll wait here for you. You talk to Mr. Landon alone and then we'll go finish our errands."

Tim licked his lips and twisted his toe into the carpet. Finally he nodded, but Wren could tell he wasn't happy with the arrangement.

The phone rang and Mrs. Tebra answered in her pleasant, well-trained voice. When she hung up, she stood and smiled at Tim. A whiff of her delicate perfume hung in the air. "Mr. Landon will be in his office in another moment. I'm going to step out to run a quick errand for him, but I'll be right back."

When the door closed behind her and her whiff of expensive perfume, Wren leaped up and turned on Bess and Paula. "How dare you follow us!"

Paula laughed and slapped her leg. "You and Tim thought you were really smart trying to sneak out the back way. I told Bess that's what you'd do, so we hid behind Mrs. Wheeler's house and watched your back door."

"It was easy to follow you because you didn't expect us to be so smart," said Bess.

Wren flipped her hair back. Fresh anger made it hard to speak. "Well, we don't have time for games right now. Tim and I have business with Mr. Landon. You girls leave."

"Oh sure," said Bess. "And leave you to do what you want. We're here on an important mission and we're going to accomplish it."

Paula giggled. "Bess, you're beginning to sound more and more like Wren. Maybe you should be the detective and let Wren be whatever it is you are."

"Maybe," said Bess.

Just then the inner door opened and Adam Landon

stood there. His eyes widened and he rubbed a hand over his jaw. "What have we here?"

Paula jumped up. "We came to see you on business."

Mr. Landon frowned at Tim. "What's going on here, Tim?"

Wren pushed Tim forward. "Go in and tell him. We'll wait here." Wren stepped in front of Bess and Paula and tried to keep them back.

Tim shook his head. "No. I can't, Wren." His face was white and he trembled. "You come with me."

"I will," said Paula, pushing past Wren.

"Me, too," said Bess, stepping out on the other side of Wren.

Mr. Landon held up a hand. "Hold it! Tim, this is a business office, not a playground."

"I know," whispered Tim.

"He came here to discuss something important," Wren said. "Please, take him to your office and talk there. It's very important."

Mr. Landon motioned to Tim. "Come along, Tim. I don't have all day."

Tim backed away, his face pale. "I'm going home."

Wren pushed him forward again while she peeked around his arm. "Tell him, Tim! What I told him yesterday was the truth!"

"Then you might as well save your breath." Mr. Landon flipped back his jacket and stood with his hands on his hips. " Mr. Humphrey explained in detail about the little misunderstanding. He said he caught you two going through my desk. He said you made up that wild tale to get back at him.

Wren gasped in horror. "We did not go through your desk! Did we, Tim?"

Bess stepped forward in her best proper manner. "Mr. Landon, my name is Bess Talbot. I'm Wren's neighbor and there's something that I think you should know about her." Bess took a deep breath. "Wren always finds a mystery even when there isn't one."

"Bess!" Wren fell back a step.

Bess turned to Wren. "Well, it's true."

"Is it, Tim?" asked Mr. Landon.

Tim frowned, and finally nodded. "But not all the time. Honest!"

Wren wanted to say not most of the time, but she truthfully couldn't say that. Most of the time she was wrong about a mystery. "I am not wrong about Humphrey!"

Mr. Landon stepped forward. Wren could smell his aftershave. "Run on home, kids. I don't have time for any of this." Mr. Landon squeezed Tim's shoulder, but Tim jerked away. "Tim, come see me alone sometime, but don't bring your friends here for games of any kind."

Wren ran to the door and pressed her back against it. "Nobody's leaving this room until the truth is told!"

"Now, little girl, don't be dramatic." Adam Landon

walked slowly across the room and stopped just inches from Wren. He bent down to her and she could smell peppermint on his breath. "Get away from the door and go home where you belong."

Wren crossed her arms and stubbornly shook her head.

Mr. Landon easily lifted her up and set her down away from the door. She felt like a baby. He opened the door, waited until Mrs. Tebra walked in, then said, "All right, kids, everyone out. Right now! I mean it. I wouldn't want to drag you all screaming to the front door and toss you out on the steps." He laughed, but Wren could tell that he was serious about them leaving. "It would give my business a bad name."

Her face red, Wren slowly walked out first, the others close behind her. Mr. Landon was going to have a client stolen from him and there was nothing she could do about it. She might as well give up.

A tear sparkled in her eye, but she wouldn't let it fall.

8

CAUGHT

Out in the reception area, Wren bit her bottom lip and narrowed her eyes. The time for embarrassment and being sorry for her mistakes was past. It was time to jump in with both feet and help Adam Landon whether he wanted help or not.

"Just who is Humphrey?" asked Paula with a scowl.

"Is he Tim's dad?" asked Bess.

Tim jabbed Bess in the shoulder. "What a dumb thing to ask."

Bess rubbed her shoulder. "What's so dumb about it?"

"Who is Humphrey?" asked Paula impatiently.

Tim gripped Wren's arm and whispered, "Look! He's in the elevator!"

Wren trembled. "What'll we do?"

"Why are you scared?" asked Paula.

"Wren?" Bess looked helplessly at Wren. "What's wrong? You're scaring me."

"Let's get out of here!" Wren shot a look around. "The

stair door! Quick! Before he gets off the elevator."

Tim led the way to the door marked Stairs with Wren right behind him and Bess and Paula in the rear. Just before they reached it, Janice dodged around them and blocked their way.

"Where do you think you're going?" she asked, leaning against the door.

"We're trying to leave," said Wren.

"Not yet," said Janice. She smiled but Wren could tell that the smile didn't reach her eyes. "I have something for you from Mr. Landon."

"We were just in his office," said Tim.

"I know. He called and said to stop you and take you to another office for him. He has a surprise for all of you. He's sorry for sending you away so abruptly."

Wren glanced over her shoulder. The elevator stood empty. Mr. Humphrey wasn't in sight. She shivered. "I think we'd better leave."

"I'm not leaving," said Paula. "I want to see what Mr. Landon has for us."

Wren's brain whirled. Something was wrong, but what? Before she could think of anything concrete, Janice hurried the others down the hall and into a small office. Against her better judgment, Wren followed. She looked around to find that there were no windows in the office. A conference table with eight, high-backed leather chairs around it stood in the center of the room. Paintings hung on the walls and two lights with several bulbs in each light hung from the ceiling over the table.

"Have a chair, kids," said Janice firmly. She tugged her sweater vest down over her skirt. "Mr. Landon will be here shortly." She stood at the door and waited until the children sat at the table. "Mr. Landon wants to give you all something special. Something very special. Please wait here until he comes in."

Wren saw the furtive look on Janice's face when she opened the door and stepped out. Before the door closed Wren saw Humphrey join Janice. Wren moved restlessly. The hair on the back of her neck stood on end. "I wonder what's going on."

"Mr. Landon wants to give us something," said Paula. She leaned her elbows on the table and looked very smug.

"I don't like this," said Tim.

"Like what?" asked Bess.

"Adam said he didn't want kids around." Tim walked to the door. "You girls can stay if you want, but I'm leaving right now."

Wren ran to his side. "I'm going with you."

Tim grabbed the doorknob and tried to turn it, but it wouldn't turn.

Wren pushed him aside. "Let me do it." She gripped the shiny knob and twisted. Her hand slipped on the knob, but it didn't turn. She looked at Tim and he looked at her. "We're locked in," whispered Wren in a strangled voice.

"Locked in," mouthed Tim.

Paula jumped off her chair. "Will you two stop playing games? Why should anyone lock us in?"

"Because of what we know," said Wren. Bess trembled as she slowly walked behind her chair. "I'll try that door," she whispered, pointing to a door on the left of the table. She looked helplessly at Wren. "It might not be locked."

Bess ran to it, but the knob wouldn't move. She turned, her face white. "We are locked in," she cried. "But why?"

"I want out of here now!" shouted Paula with her head back and her mouth opened wide. "Let me out or I'll call my dad!"

"Help!" Tim cupped his hands around his mouth and shouted again. "Help! We're locked in!"

Wren looked expectantly toward the door, but it didn't open. "The room must be soundproof or someone would've come to see what the shouting was all about."

"Oh, no," said Bess with her hand at her throat.

Wren ran to the door that led into the hallway and knocked on it with both fists. Her sweater felt tight around her throat. She waited, but nothing happened. "Tim, how could someone not hear us? Janice would, wouldn't she?"

"She locked us in here, so why should she want to help us get out?" Tim leaned against the door and looked at Wren. "We'll have to think like pros and not let our circumstances stop our thinking. We have to find a way out before everyone leaves for the day. We don't want to be locked in here all night."

"All night!" Bess dropped to a chair and covered her ashen face with trembling hands.

Paula swallowed hard. She rubbed her hands down her jeans. "My parents won't allow me to stay away the entire night. They're probably sending out a search team right now." She sank to a chair and propped her elbows on the table, her chin in her hands.

"You should've stayed home," said Tim.

Bess glared at Paula. "It's all your fault. I told you to find something else for us to do today since we're best friends now."

Wren's stomach knotted. She had lost Bess as a best friend. Now, who would talk with her about Brian Davies? She bit her lip. This wasn't the time to think about that. They had to find a way out.

With Tim at her side, she walked slowly to first one door and then another and tried to think of a plan while Bess and Paula argued about whose fault it was that they were in trouble.

"We could try to take out the hinges," said Tim.

Wren pulled on the lowest hinge, but couldn't budge it. "That won't work."

"How about breaking down the door?"

"Too solid. Unless we beat on it with a chair."

69

Wren turned to study the chairs, but each chair was a heavy arm chair with leather upholstery. She ran to the nearest chair and struggled to lift it, but couldn't. Only when Tim stood on one side and they lifted together could they move it. Panting, Wren said, "That won't work either."

Tim leaned against the high back of the chair. "We'll have to think of a plan."

"What plan?" asked Paula.

"A plan to get us out," said Wren. "I don't want to get hurt," wailed Bess.

"I'd like to know why we're locked in," said Paula.

Wren took a deep breath. "Tim and I overheard Geoff Humphrey making plans to steal a wealthy client from Adam Landon. Humphrey knows we heard him and he wants to shut us up."

"For good?" asked Bess, shivering with fear.

"I hope not," said Wren.

"I'm too young to die," said Paula, whimpering.

"We're not going to die," said Tim sharply. "It would be too hard to explain the deaths of four kids."

Wren nodded, "I think they're trying to keep us away from Mr. Landon until Humphrey can steal Sid from the agency. If I'm right, they'll come for us soon, so we have to find a way to escape. Let's think of a plan."

They huddled together in a corner near the door and discussed first one way and then another.

Finally Wren said, "I have it!"

70

"What?" asked Tim.

"What?" asked Bess.

"Tell us," said Paula.

Wren tipped back her head and laughed. "This is perfect, just perfect, but we'll all have to cooperate."

"I don't know if I can do anything," said Bess.

"I'll try anything," said Paula.

"What's your plan, Wren?" asked Tim.

"We'll turn the table on its side and slide it into Humphrey when he comes for us."

"But he'll see it and move," said Paula. "We'll take out the light bulbs to make the room dark," said Tim, his eyes sparkling. "They won't see what we're planning."

"What door will they come in?" asked Bess.

Wren frowned. "That's a good question?"

"We'll hook a chair under the knob to that door so it can't be opened," said Tim, pointing to the inside door. He tugged a chair across the carpet with Wren's help and tipped it up under the knob. He stepped back with a satisfied smile. "That'll do it."

"I think we're too smart for Humphrey," said Wren. "He'll be expecting just a bunch of dumb kids and he'll find us." She laughed and the others joined in. "Let's pull the chairs away from the table."

While the girls moved the chairs, Tim jumped up on the table and unscrewed the light bulbs just enough that they went out. The room was pitched into darkness.

"I don't like the dark!" cried Paula. "Leave one light on."

"We don't dare," said Wren.

"I'm done," said Tim. "Grab the table and let's turn it up on its side. It'll move easily across the carpet when we push it."

"Hurry," said Wren. "We don't know how much time we have." She felt the table and heard the others move into place. "One, two, three, tip!" She heaved and the table moved and tipped and flipped all the way over to land on the floor with a loud thud. Bess and Paula screamed, Tim cried out and Wren said, "Oh, no!"

"Hurry! We have to lift it!" said Tim.

Wren moved into place and bumped into Bess. "You stay here, Bess, and I'll move down a little."

"I wish I would've stayed home," whispered Bess. "I'm scared."

"God is with us," said Wren. "Don't forget that."

"That's right, Wren. Now, everybody ready?" asked Tim. "When I say lift. One, two, three, lift."

Wren strained and the table moved. Her arms ached and perspiration popped out on her forehead. Finally the table teetered, steadied and stood on its side. "Hang on tight so it doesn't fall again. Tim, you move around to the back. Paula, you come up here by the front. Bess, you go down near Tim and I'll stay up here."

Wren's mouth turned dry. What if the plan didn't work?

"I hope we don't have to stand here holding up this table all night long," said Paula.

"Will we?" asked Bess.

"They'll come," said Tim. "They can't leave us here forever."

Wren leaned her forehead against the table. Would they leave them forever? "Let's try it and see if it does move easily. One, two, three, go!"

The table skimmed over the carpet and they stopped just inches from the door. Carefully they moved back about a couple of feet.

Just then Wren heard a movement at the door. Her heart plunged to her feet. "Ready, everyone," she hissed. "I think they're coming."

The doorknob rattled and Wren shivered.

9

ESCAPE

Silence filled the room and Wren was sure everyone could hear the wild thud of her heart. Her sweater and jeans felt hot against her thin body. Her feet burned inside her tennis shoes.

"I'm going to faint," whispered Bess.

"No, you're not," hissed Wren.

The doorknob rattled again, then all was silent.

"I guess it wasn't Humphrey," said Wren in a weak voice.

"I am going to let go of this table and scream," said Paula.

"No!" cried Tim.

"You can't. This won't work if we don't all work together. The table is too heavy. If you let go, the rest of us couldn't hold it."

"You're important, Paula," said Bess.

Paula was silent for a few seconds. "It's time you all realized it."

Just then the doorknob rattled again and Wren said, "Shhh! Get ready."

The door opened. A man blocked the doorway. "What's wrong with the lights? Where are you kids?" It was Humphrey.

Wren trembled and bit her lip to keep from crying out.

"What happened to them?" asked Janice in alarm.

"They're hiding," said Humphrey. "Come on, kids. We're taking you for a ride." He walked into the room with Janice behind him.

"Go!" cried Wren. She pushed along with the others and the table glided easily over the carpet, crashing into Humphrey. With a cry of pain he fell back and knocked against Janice. They both sprawled to the floor with loud, angry shouts.

"Let go!" cried Tim.

Wren let go of the table just as the others did. Together they ran forward. As the table crashed to the floor, they reached the doorway.

Humphrey reached out and grabbed Tim's ankle.

"Hey! Let me go!"

Wren stopped and turned while Bess and Paula kept running. She kicked Humphrey's elbow, making him cry out.

Tim jerked free and ran.

Bess and Paula reached the elevator and Paula held it

open while they all dashed inside. Bess pushed the button and the door slid closed just before Humphrey and Janice reached it.

"We made it," said Wren, leaning weakly against the shiny bar. But she had seen the anger on Humphrey's face and she trembled. How she wanted to go home and sit on the couch beside Dad and listen to him talk about his day.

"Look down there." Tim pointed down and Wren saw Sid standing near the outer door. Her heart zoomed to her feet.

"Who is it?" asked Bess, peering down.

"The client Humphrey is stealing," said Wren. Suddenly she felt too tired to move. "What'll we do now?"

"He sees us!" cried Paula.

"Is he going to hurt us?" Bess clutched Wren's arm with trembling, cold hands.

"We won't give him a chance." Tim jabbed the second floor button and the elevator slid to a stop, one floor above Sid.

Wren ran out with the others behind her. She stumbled, caught herself and sped down the hallway, then suddenly exclaimed, "Tim, no one's in the building."

"Maybe it's already closing time," he said.

Paula looked at her watch. "It's four thirty."

"The offices all close at four," said Tim.

"I'm scared," whispered Bess.

"Sid will be up here after us," said Wren. "We'll have to

think of something fast." Frantically she looked around the hall. "Tim, is there a phone around?"

"I don't know. In an office, I guess." He dashed to the first door and tried it, but it didn't open. He tried all of them, but none opened except the stair door. "What're we going to do now?"

Wren looked anxiously at the stair door. Would Sid step through the door any second and capture them again? "Let's get back to the elevator."

Tim jabbed the down button and a century later the door slid open. They jumped inside and Tim hesitated and looked helplessly at Wren. "Up or down?"

She peered down and couldn't see anyone. "Down. I think."

"I want to go home," said Bess with a sob.

"So do I," said Paula. Tears filled her eyes and she turned and wiped them away.

The door slid open and Wren cautiously stepped out. A chill ran up and down her spine. "I don't see anyone," she whispered.

"I'm scared." Bess pressed closed to Wren.

"We have to hurry!" cried Tim. He raced to the door with the girls on his heels. He pushed on the door but it didn't budge. He tried again and Wren helped him, then Bess and Paula pushed, too.

Wren slumped against the door. "Locked!"

"I give up," said Paula with a sob she didn't try to hide.

"I'll never forgive you, Wren House."

"We can't give up," said Tim as he looked around. Wren stood beside Tim, silently praying for help.

Bess frantically tugged Wren's arm. "Look! Oh, look!"

Wren turned to find the elevator slipping down toward them with Humphrey, Janice, and Sid inside. "Oh, no!" Wren watched until the elevator was almost to the first floor. "Follow me!" In a flash Wren ran to the stairs with the others behind her. At the second floor, she turned to run up to the third floor, then stopped to look out the window.

"Mr. Landon! Look! He's getting out of his car and heading this way!"

"We're saved!" cried Paula.

"No! Look!" Tim pointed out the stairway door to the elevator just as its door slid open.

"Head down again!" screamed Wren over a loud wail from Bess.

Together they raced down the stairs, shouting, "Mr. Landon! Help! Help!"

Above them they heard the door slam and heavy footsteps clambered after them.

"Follow me!" cried Tim.

"Come back here, you kids!" shouted Humphrey as he ran down the stairs.

Her mouth like cotton, Wren followed Tim, Bess and Paula to the bottom of the stairway and out into the lobby.

"Adam!" called Tim. "Help us!"

Adam Landon rounded a corner, and Wren watched Tim run right into him.

"What's going on here?" asked Adam with a scowl, holding Tim from him. "Why are you kids here? How did you get back in?"

"We never left," said Paula.

"We were locked in," said Bess.

Wren and Tim both talked at once as they tried to explain about Humphrey. Finally Adam held up a hand.

"Hold it! You all look frightened and you're not making any sense. Calm down and only one of you talk. Tim."

Wren glanced over her shoulder just in time to see Humphrey duck out of sight. "There he is!"

"Quiet!" Adam scowled at her. Wren snapped her mouth closed. "Tim, start talking. Now!"

With a shaky voice Tim told their story and Adam interrupted from time to time with a question. When Tim finished, Adam shook his head and tugged his tie loose.

"You kids have been watching too much TV."

Wren stuck out her chin and crossed her arms. "We can prove it happened."

"We'll show you the room where we were locked up." Tim marched down the hall toward the elevator, his face set with determination.

Bess and Paula hung back, their faces white. "We don't

want to go up there," said Paula.

"Stop playing games," snapped Adam. "We'll all go up and look and then go from there." He strode ahead to the elevator and jabbed the up button. The only sound was Bess sniffing back tears until the swish of the elevator broke the spell. Tim once again tried to convince Adam that they were telling the truth.

"Not another word until we see the room," said Adam, shaking a finger at Tim. Adam held the door while the others entered, then he stepped inside and pushed the button. He moved back and jangled keys and change in his pockets. The scent of his aftershave blended with an old perfume smell that lingered in the elevator.

Finally the door opened and Wren rushed out. She ran down the hall with the others following. She looked around, then finally spotted the door to the room where they'd been prisoners only moments before. "This room!" She pointed dramatically at the door.

"Right inside there," said Tim, pointing also.

Bess and Paula nodded.

"Impossible," said Adam. He tried the knob, but it didn't turn. "That door is locked."

"Don't you have a key?" asked Wren.

"Of course." Adam reached in his pocket and pulled out a key. He unlocked the door and Wren shot a knowing look at Tim.

"The lights don't work," said Tim. "I unscrewed the

bulbs."

Adam clicked the switch and light flooded the room. He stepped inside with the others pushing in behind him. "Just as I thought," he said grimly.

Wren's eyes widened as she looked at the room. The table with eight chairs around it stood neatly in the center of the room just as it had before they'd tipped it up.

"This is impossible! Tim ran to the first chair and touched it as if to assure himself that it was really there. He turned helplessly to Wren.

She stood very still as her heart sank slowly to her feet.

"I'm going to call your parents and we're going to get to the bottom of this prank," said Adam.

"Don't bother calling my parents," said Tim coldly.

Wren held her breath.

"What do you mean by that?" asked Adam.

Tim doubled his fists at his sides. "Forget it. Nothing at all. But it won't do any good to call Mom."

Paula stepped forward, her hands clasped in front of her. "Please, don't call my parents. My dad is a doctor and he doesn't like it when I get in trouble."

Wren said, "How can you think we're lying, Mr. Landon? We aren't! We're telling the truth. We were locked in that room by Janice."

Adam shook his head. "No more of this nonsense."

Wren opened her mouth, but he tapped her shoulder with his finger and she snapped her lips shut.

Adam took a deep breath. "I won't call your parents this time, but if you kids ever come here again to play your silly games, I will. Now, go home."

"We can't go anywhere until you unlock the door to let us out," said Wren.

Adam nodded. "You're right. Let's go."

Wren hesitated, darting looks around. Finally she ran after the others and slipped inside the elevator. She wouldn't say anything now, but she would not give up until Humphrey was exposed. She glanced at Tim but he was staring straight ahead, his face set. She bit her bottom lip and waited for the elevator door to open.

10

THE THREAT

Adam Landon held the outside door. A gentle breeze blew in, cooling Wren's hot face. Cars drove past and one honked.

"Are you sure it's safe?" asked Bess, peering around with wide blue eyes before she stepped outdoors.

Adam frowned. "It's safe." He sounded impatient.

"Are you sure?" asked Paula, lingering in the doorway.

Adam sighed heavily. "I'm sure. I'm really getting tired of this. Get out so I can get on with my business." His face softened. "Kids, I don't want to sound mean, but I don't have time for your pranks. Go play with someone your own age. I'm thirty years old and I'm too old and too busy for this."

"It's not a game," said Wren, lifting her chin and looking squarely into Adam's face.

"It's not," said Tim.

Adam narrowed his eyes and slowly nodded. "If it'll make you all feel better, I'll be on my guard."

"Good," said Wren.

"I'm going to be on my guard, too," said Bess, glaring at Paula. "I won't let you talk me into tracking down Tim's dad."

Tim sucked in his breath and Wren froze.

"What about Tim's dad?" asked Adam.

"Nothing," said Wren quickly.

"Nothing," echoed Tim just above a whisper.

Paula flipped back her hair and faced Adam. "Tim found out yesterday that his dad lives right here in town and he knows who he is. He won't tell us who it is but I want to know and so does Bess."

"I don't want to know any longer," said Bess. "I don't even care that Tim knows."

Wren's stomach fluttered. Adam bent down to Tim. "Do you know, Tim?" he asked softly.

A muscle jumped in Tim's jaw. Finally he nodded.

"Let's talk about it." Adam clamped a hand on Tim's shoulder, but Tim jerked free.

Wren cleared her throat. "Tim, you stay and talk and I'll ride home with Bess and Paula."

"I don't want to stay," whispered Tim hoarsely.

"Stay anyway," said Adam. "I can help you. I promise."

Wren watched Tim's face turn red, then white; at last, he nodded. She smiled a small quivery smile. "I'll talk to you later. Call me when you get home."

Tim barely tipped his head to let her know he would.

"We'll go to my office," said Adam. He looked pale

and unsure of himself.

"Let's go, girls." Wren ran down the steps toward the bikes. At the bottom of the steps she turned. Tim and Adam stood inside the Landon building looking at each other. Butterflies fluttered in Wren's stomach. She glanced at Bess and Paula as they lifted their bikes up. Did they suspect anything? They seemed too anxious to get home to think of suspecting Adam Landon of being Tim's dad. Wren wanted to dash back to Tim and stay by his side while he talked with Adam, but she picked up her bike instead.

A few minutes later Wren pedaled down the street with Bess beside her and Paula just behind. They stopped at a red light. The smell of fried chicken drifted out of the Chicken Coop and Wren's stomach cramped with hunger.

Just then a car pulled up beside them. Wren turned to glance at the driver and her blood froze in her veins. It was Humphrey and he looked very angry as his window slipped down. She shivered.

Humphrey stuck his head out the window. Sparks shot from his eyes and his nostrils flared. "If you kids know what's good for you, you'll stay away from Adam Landon. If you don't, I'll contact your parents and tell them that you have been harassing people at the Landon Building. And if that doesn't stop you, I'll sue your parents for the trouble you've caused me." The light turned green and he drove away in his black Cadillac.

"Now what, Wren?" asked Paula with a sob.

"I'm scared," said Bess, shivering.

Wren couldn't speak as she led the way to the sidewalk. She sagged against the corner of the library and looked at the girls beside her. "I am going to stop that man," she said through clenched teeth.

Bess shook her head. "No! No, don't try anything, Wren. He means what he said!"

"My dad will be so angry!" cried Paula. "I don't want him to yell at me."

Wren narrowed her eyes. Now that she was over the shock her brain was working again. "How can he tell our parents anything? He doesn't know who we are. We didn't tell him. Or Janice."

"I said my dad's a doctor."

"But there are lots of doctors in town. Is he going to call each one and ask if he has a daughter?"

"He might," said Bess, shivering.

"He won't." Wren stood her bike up and gripped the handlebars. "Let's go. Maybe I'll come up with a plan tomorrow." For now she had to get home to wait beside the phone for Tim to call. "We'll stay close together all the way home and nothing will happen to us."

Bess looked around, smoothed back her blonde hair and straddled her bike. "I'll ever leave my house again."

"I don't think I'll try to be a detective ever again," said Paula. "It's a dangerous job."

Wren didn't say anything as she led the way to Lyons

Street. Several minutes later as she stood in her own kitchen and drank a tall glass of cold water, she felt the peace and safety around her. She knew her dad was in his office with a client; Neil was in his room; and her mom had left a note saying that she'd gone to get a few groceries.

Wren slowly walked to the kitchen table and sat in the spot where she always sat for a meal. She rubbed the outside of her glass and thought about everything that had happened since she'd left at noon. The afternoon seemed three days long.

She looked toward the silent telephone. "Tim. Oh, Tim, what's happening to you right now?"

"Talking to yourself, Wren?"

She turned her head and her face lit up. "Hi, Dad."

Sam House walked to the sink and filled a glass with water. He dropped a couple of ice cubes in it from the freezer and sat across from Wren. His brown eyes were filled with love as he looked at Wren. "What's up with Tim?"

Wren bit her bottom lip. "Do you want to hear about my day?"

"I always want to hear about your day."

So, she told him. She finished her story with, "I'm going to find a way to stop Humphrey."

Sam shook his head. "You'd better let me handle that, Wren. It sounds like Humphrey is out to play with the big boys. He might hurt you, and I can't let that happen."

She thought about that for a minutes, then finally

nodded. "But maybe we could work together." One of her biggest dreams was to be a detective in his agency.

"Maybe."

"Really?"

Sam winked. "Aren't you the best? Next to me, of course?"

She laughed and felt warm all over. "Am I really?"

"Sure. For your age. Get a few more years under your belt and you'll be right there at the top."

"Thanks, Dad." She glowed with the thought, then sobered as she thought of Tim. "Tim might be able to convince Mr. Landon that we told him the truth now that he knows that Tim knows that he knows that he's his son."

Sam tipped back his head and laughed. "I don't know if I know if you know what you just said."

"I know." She giggled.

"And I know." Sam laughed and reached over and squeezed Wren's hand.

They talked for several more minutes about Humphrey and Adam Landon and Tim. Finally Wren jumped up.

"I can't wait another minute. Tim hasn't called yet! I have to talk to him. Dad, I want to ride to his house and see if he's all right."

Sam glanced at the gold watch at his wrist. "It's almost dinner time."

"I have to know that he's all right, and I can't call him. He turns off his phone."

"Why?"

"Because of his mom. He's afraid she'd answer it and embarrass him if it's one of his friends."

"I could drive you over right now."

She ran to him and flung herself into his arms. "Would you? Thank you!"

"I'll tell Neil."

A few minutes later they drove up to Tim's house. Wren opened her door. A cool wind blew in and Wren was glad that she'd grabbed her jacket. "I won't be long, Dad."

"Have him come for dinner if you want."

"Thanks."

She ran to the door and knocked. She waited and knocked again. No sound came from inside the house. She ran around to where Tim left his bike. It wasn't there. Her heart sank. She dashed to the car and slipped inside. "He's not there, Dad. He should be home by now."

"Maybe he's still with Adam Landon. We'll drive past the Landon Building and see if his bike is there."

Wren clutched her seat belt and stared straight ahead as Dad drove. Outside the Landon Building she looked for Tim's bike. "It's not there, either, Dad. Drive around to the side of the building and let's see if Mr. Landon's car is still here."

Sam pulled away from the curb and drove around the corner. Adam Landon's white Mercedes sat where he'd parked it.

Wren's heart sank. "Oh, Dad! Where is Tim? Do you think Humphrey found him alone and grabbed him?"

"I wouldn't worry about Tim. He can take care of himself," said Sam. "He could be anywhere."

"You're right, of course." With a heavy sigh Wren leaned back against the soft fabric of the seat.

"I'll tell you what, Wren," her dad said, squeezing her cold hand, "we'll drive around and if we see Tim we'll talk to him."

"Thanks, Dad."

He winked and smiled.

She watched out her window as Dad drove slowly up one street and down another. She saw two boys from her class and many people that she didn't know, but she didn't see Tim.

After several blocks Sam turned down Madison toward Lyons. "It's time to give up and go home, Wren."

"All right, but I hate to. I feel like something's wrong." She pressed her hand to her stomach. "I feel it right here."

"I've had that feeling when I've been working on a case. Sometimes, you can follow that feeling and other times you have to give up and give it time and space."

"He'll probably call me later today or tomorrow." Her stomach growled. "Maybe it's just hunger. I am hungry."

Where was Tim right now? Was he alone, scared, hungry and Humphrey's prisoner? She sighed loud and long. "Let's go home, Dad."

11

A VERY LONG WEEKEND

On Saturday morning Wren flipped a clean yellow sheet onto her bed, pulled all four corners over each edge, shook out the clean top sheet and put it in place. Just as she tucked in the bottom she heard a sound and lifted her head. Had the phone rung? She ran to the door and stuck her head out the door. She heard Neil whistling in his room and Philip talking to Dad while he cleaned the bathroom. The phone wasn't ringing. With a sigh she walked back to her bed to put the blankets in place.

"Tim just has to call this morning! He has to!"

She stood with her pillow hugged to her, the clean case on the carpet beside her. Had Humphrey kidnapped Tim yesterday? She shivered at the terrible thought.

Lorrene House poked her head in Wren's bedroom doorway. Her mom was dressed in jeans and a sweatshirt and looked totally different than she did when she dressed in a business suit to go to court. "Finished, Wren?"

Wren grabbed the pillowcase. "Almost, Mom."

"Is something wrong, Wren?"

Wren hesitated. Mom hated it when she did detective work. "I'm waiting for a call from Tim. He was supposed to call last night, and didn't."

"He's probably busy with his Saturday morning chores."

"I don't think so, Mom." Tim didn't do Saturday morning chores. His house was usually a mess and he never had to clean it.

Lorrene shrugged. She tucked her shoulder length strawberry blond hair behind her ears. "Finish up and we'll go to the mall and get new shoes for you. I can't believe you've outgrown your new ones already."

"Mom, I was nine when you bought them."

"You were? Time really sails past, doesn't it?"

"It does?" Wren felt like she'd already lived an entire week in two days. Twice she'd called Amos Pike to ask about Tim. Amos hadn't seen him.

Lorrene leaned against the doorway. "I think I'll see if we can find a new skirt for you, too."

"I don't want to be gone long, Mom."

"Why not?"

"Tim might call."

"Oh, Wren. Is there something you're not telling me?"

Wren kept silent.

"You're involved in another mystery."

"Why do you say that?"

"I see that look in your eye. I've been trained to read

people and I can read you easily. I know there's something going on." Lorrene took a deep breath. "Does your father know what it is?"

Wren fingered the bottom of her sweatshirt. "Yes."

"And does it have something to do with a mystery?"

"Yes."

"Then I'll let him handle it. I don't think I want to know." Lorrene hugged Wren close. "I love you, honey, but I really wish you'd stop playing detective."

"I'm not playing, Mother. I am a detective." Wren locked her hands together in front of her. "Dad's a detective and you love him."Lorrene smoothed down Wren's brown hair. "I love you, too, Wren, but just because I love you doesn't mean that we can't disagree on things."

"Oh, Wren." Lorrene kissed the top of Wren's brown hair. "I want so much for you, Wren. Before you were born I prayed for a baby girl. We already had two boys, but I wanted a little girl. When you were born I was so happy! So happy that I cried. I don't cry easily, but I did when I heard I had a baby girl. And I cried when I held you in my arms and saw your little red face and black, black hair."

Wren had never heard this story before. It made her feel all soft and warm inside. She touched her mom's hand. "Oh, Mom."

"I couldn't believe the doctor when he said you were a girl. I named you a special name, a name that would leap out at people so that no one would ever forget you."

Wren grinned. "No one does, Mom."

"I guess I wanted you to be something ladylike—a prima ballerina or a concert pianist."

"But I want to be a detective."

"I know you do and that's what upsets me. A detective faces too much danger."

Wren looked up at Mom with wide brown eyes. "I wish I could be what you want, Mom, but I can't."

Lorrene sighed heavily. "I know. But I can't stop wishing, can I?"

"I guess not."

"I want you to have a nice, safe career." Mom smiled. "Finish your work and get ready to go shopping. Maybe we can stop at Tim's house and see why he hasn't called."

"Thanks, Mom." Wren wrapped her arms around Lorrene's slender waist and hugged her as tight as she could. "I love you."

"I love you, too." Lorrene kissed Wren's cheek, smiled and left to get dressed.

The phone rang and Wren jumped, her heart racing. "Tim," she whispered. She heard Dad answer as she raced down the hall and slid to a stop.

Sam held out the white receiver. "It's for you."

"Thanks." She grabbed the receiver. "Tim, why didn't you call sooner?"

"Wren, it's me," said Bess in a cold voice. "I should

hang up, but I won't."

Wren sagged against the chair near the phone. "Sorry, Bess. Tim hasn't called and I'm scared that something happened."

"Tim can take care of himself. He always does."

"I guess so."

"I didn't call to talk about Tim."

Wren twisted the white cord. "Why did you call?"

Bess was silent for a minute. "Is Carin there right now?"

"Carin?"

"Shhh! She might hear you."

Wren looked around with a frown. "She's not here."

"I saw her walk past my house. I thought she was going to see Neil. Are you sure she's not there?"

"I'm not positive, but I don't think so. Should I go see?"

"Yes, but don't be obvious. I don't want them to know that I want to know. Let them think that you want to know."

"I'll be very careful." Wren laid the receiver down on the table and ran to Neil's room. His door was open and she stuck her head in. He had finished cleaning his room and was alone.

"What'd you want?" Neil turned from dusting off his computer. "You can't tell me it's my turn to help with lunch."

Wren shook her head. "I just wondered if you'd seen Carin today."

"Carin?"

"Carin Johns."

"Oh, her. No, I haven't seen her today. Why do you ask?"

Wren shrugged. "I just wondered."

Neil balled up the dust rag and pitched it into the small wicker clothesbasket in the corner of his room. The rag landed neatly inside and Neil leaped high with a cheer and clicked his heels together. "I've still got it." He twirled around and dropped to the chair in front of his computer.

Wren ran back to the phone. "She's not here."

Bess sighed in relief. "Is she going to visit Neil today?"

"I don't know."

"Didn't you ask?"

"I didn't think of it, Bess."

"Didn't think of it! I can't believe it!" Bess suddenly grew quiet. "I wonder where she was going? If she does come to your house, will you let me know?"

"Yes. I'll call you."

"Are you going to be home all day?"

"No, I'm going to the mall with Mom to get a pair of shoes."

"Then you won't know if Carin comes or not."

"I'll tell Neil to let you know."

"Don't you dare! I won't speak to you ever again if you say anything to Neil about me asking about Carin!"

"I was only teasing."

"Well, don't tease about such important things."

"I've got to go now, Bess. I'll talk to you later."

"All right. Just don't forget."

"I won't."

"You might get so busy thinking about Tim that you'll forget all about me."

"I won't." Wren promised as she said goodbye again and hung up. Several minutes later she slipped into the car beside her mom and they drove away from the house.

"We'll check on Tim first so that you won't be worried while we're shopping."

"Thanks, Mom."

But Tim wasn't home and neither was his mother. The house was locked and looked very empty and deserted. Tim's bike wasn't there either. Wren walked back to the car with a long face and slow steps. She sank down in the passenger seat. "He's not there."

"We'll check again after we're done shopping," said Lorrene, patting Wren's jean clad leg.

"I can't understand why he's not home or why he didn't call."

"He'll have a good explanation when he finally calls."

Wren leaned back against the seat and closed her eyes as her mom drove to the mall. When the car stopped Wren turned in her seat. "Mom, what if Tim was kidnapped?"

"Don't do this, Wren. Who would kidnap him? He's not a wealthy boy, you know."

"You don't understand, Mom."

"Does your dad?"

"Yes."

"Then let him handle it with you. You and I are going to have fun shopping and not think about anything else. All right?"

"All right." Wren slipped out of the car into the bright sunshine. It was hard to imagine that in just another month the entire parking lot could be full of snow drifts.

At the end of the car she caught a glimpse of a red headed boy. "Tim!" she shouted.

The boy turned, but it wasn't Tim. Her shoulders sagged as she slowly walked toward her mom.

12

A SURPRISE VISIT

Wren bit into Dad's special fried chicken. She heard the crunch of the crisp coating as if it came from a great distance and felt the heat of the moist meat without really tasting it. She chewed slowly as she stared across the dining room at a picture of apples on the wall.

"Doesn't it taste good, Wren?" asked Sam.

"Wren, where are you? asked Philip as he handed her the bowl of leafy tossed salad.

"Wren." Lorrene nudged her. "Wren."

Wren shook herself as if she'd just awoke from a long sleep. "Did somebody say something to me?"

Neil laughed. "Wren, you're eating Dad's delicious fried chicken without tasting it. If you don't want it, give it to me." Neil was trying a new experiment. He'd grown tired of waiting for his growth spurt and so he was trying to force it by eating extra proteins and taking natural vitamins. It wasn't working.

"I do want it," said Wren. "It's my favorite." She bit off

another piece and actually tasted the juicy morsel. "It's really good, Dad."

"You ate one piece without even tasting it," said Neil.

"I did?" Wren forked up a bite of creamy mashed potatoes. She looked at it and slowly stuck it in her mouth. Why hadn't Tim called yet? He hadn't been home yesterday at all and this morning he hadn't been in Sunday School or church. Something was really wrong. She dropped her fork with a clatter.

"What's wrong now?" asked Philip. "Don't you dare try to get out of doing dishes today. I won't be here to do them for you. I'm taking Brenda to the park for the open air concert."

"I'll do the dishes," sad Wren. "I'm just thinking about Tim."

"Tim's going to be just fine," said Lorrene. "I thought you agreed to stop worrying about him after we prayed for him last night."

"I guess I did." Wren grinned sheepishly. "I forgot."

Neil pointed to a slice of peach in Wren's fruit dish. "If you aren't going to eat that, I will."

Sam tapped Neil's arm with his finger. "Neil, let your sister eat her own food."

"May I be excused?" asked Philip. "I have to brush my teeth and fix my hair before I go get Brenda."

Lorrene smiled and nodded. "Be home by five."

"I will." Philip pushed back his chair. "Brenda just

might be the love of my life."

"Don't push it," said Sam. "You're sixteen. You'll have a love of your life at least twice a week for the next few years."

Philip grinned and dashed away.

"I'm never going to spend more time with girls than I do with my computer," said Neil.

"You're thirteen," said Sam with a chuckle. "Never make a statement like that at thirteen years of age."

Wren pushed her dish of peaches to Neil. "You can have them. I can't eat any more." She turned to her dad. "I need to ride over and see about Tim."

"No," said Lorrene before Sam could answer. "It's your day for dishes."

"Please, Dad," begged Wren.

Sam and Lorrene exchanged looks and Sam said, "Do the dishes and after that, if you still want to ride to Tim's, go ahead."

"Sam," said Lorrene. "Tim won't be home. We drove past his house after church and he wasn't there."

"He might be now," said Wren.

"It's good exercise," said Sam. He walked around to Lorrene, bent down and kissed her soft cheek. "Speaking of exercise, let's you and me go for a walk after dishes. This Indian summer won't last."

Lorrene smiled, her face glowing as she looked at her husband. "A walk sounds perfect. Maybe we could walk to

Brush Creek."

Sam groaned. "That's a long way, honey. I don't know if I can handle that today."

"Whatever you say, Sam. But I think once you're walking, all of your energy will return and you'll even be able to walk around Brush Creek." Lorrene smiled up at Sam, then turned to Neil. "I want you outdoors to enjoy the day, too. You can't stay cooped up in your bedroom with your computer on such a glorious day."

Neil wrinkled his nose. "All right. I'll go see what Brian's doing." His voice cracked and he smiled proudly. He was looking forward to a deep, manly voice so that people didn't think he was Wren when he answered the phone.

Wren jumped up, her face pale. For once hearing Brian's name didn't send her pulse leaping. "We can't all leave the house at the same time! What if Tim calls?"

Lorrene picked up the leftover potatoes and the platter that had held the chicken. "Wren, you can't live your life around Tim. If he tries to call you when we're not here, he'll call back."

"We'll put on the answering machine," said Sam, ruffling Wren's hair.

Wren smiled in relief. "Thanks, Dad."

"I'll be glad when this whole business with Tim is settled," said Lorrene.

Wren picked up the forks while Lorrene walked to the

104

kitchen. "Dad, where could Tim be?"

"I don't know, Wren." Sam picked up the empty water glasses. "I'm sure you'll hear from him soon. If not today, you'll see him at school in the morning."

"I hope so." She walked to the kitchen with a heavy heart and her hands full of silverware. She rinsed them off and loaded them in the dishwasher.

Just as she finished in the kitchen, the phone rang. Her stomach cramped and she ran to answer.

"Wren, why didn't you tell me?"

At the sound of Bess's voice, Wren sagged against the counter. "Tell you what, Bess?"

"That Neil and Carin were going together."

"But they aren't!"

"I just saw them, Wren." Bess sniffed hard. "They walked right past my house."

"Neil said he was going to Brian's. Maybe Carin was out for a walk and she just happened to see Neil." Wren didn't want to talk about Neil or Carin or anyone. She wanted to get her bike and go see if Tim was home.

"I'm coming over to talk to you, Wren."

"You can't, Bess. I'm leaving."

"Leaving? Where're you going?"

Wren bit her bottom lip and gripped the receiver tighter. Finally she said, "I'm going to see if Tim's home."

"Tim! I need you and you're going to see Tim?"

"Don't be mad."

"Well, I am." Bess slammed down the receiver and the crack hurt Wren's ear.

"Please don't be mad, Bess," whispered Wren as she slowly set the receiver in place. "I have to see if Tim's safe."

Just then the front doorbell rang. Wren jumped, then dashed to answer it just as Sam and Lorrene walked into the living room dressed for their hike.

Wren flung open the door. "Tim! It's you!"

"Adam and I came to talk to you and your folks."

"May we come in?" asked Adam.

Wren nodded and stepped to one side. Adam walked past her, but she caught Tim's arm. "You didn't call!"

Tim ran a finger around the neckline of his sweater. "I . . . I'm sorry. I . . . forgot."

"Forgot?"

Tim turned away from Wren and cleared his throat. "Sam and Lorrene House, this is Adam Landon."

While her parents spoke to Adam Landon, Wren studied Tim with a frown. He wore new jeans and a new blue sweater with a white shirt under it. Instead of his old tennis shoes he wore brand new ones.

Adam turned from Lorrene and Sam and smiled at Wren. "We need to talk."

Wren flushed. "We do?"

"Don't be upset with Tim. I kept him so busy listening to me that he really didn't think to call. I'm sorry."

106

Wren nodded and slowly walked to the chair across from the couch. Something was happening and she wanted to know what. She watched Adam and Tim sit down side by side. Tim didn't seem angry with Adam, nor Adam with him. Wren glanced at her mom and dad as they sat down.

Tim leaned forward and looked right at Wren. "He believes me. About Humphrey."

"He does?" She glanced at Adam. "You do?"

"I do." Adam slipped an arm around Tim's shoulders. "We had a long talk. A very long talk." Adam took a deep breath. "Mr. and Mrs. House, Tim is my son. One of these days, when he's used to the idea, I hope he'll call me Dad."

Wren watched her parents' expressions, but she couldn't tell if they were surprised. She knew they were both experienced in hiding their feelings.

Adam patted Tim's knee and smiled reassuringly at him before he looked back at Lorrene and Sam.

"I would've told the whole town before this, but it was an awkward situation. I was very young and selfish when Heather Avery and I were married. I wasn't ready for a child and when I found out she was pregnant, I refused to be responsible for her or the baby. We divorced. Later, after I'd sorted out my life, I met and married Molly. Together we learned about God and His great love for us. We both accepted Christ as our Savior."

107

Adam glanced at Tim. "God changed my life. Then He gave me the courage to meet you and try to help you. I've tried to help your mother, but she didn't want the kind of help that I could give her." Adam flushed and looked guilty. "I couldn't change the past, and I couldn't just suddenly walk into Tim's life after all these years. Tim knows now how sorry I am for those lost years."

Tim ducked his head, but didn't speak.

"You don't owe us an explanation, Mr. Landon," said Sam.

"I know, but my son and your daughter are friends and I wanted to clear it up the best I could. I want you and Wren as well as Tim to know that I'm not ashamed of Tim."

Wren fingered the arm rest of her chair.

Adam patted Tim's hand. "Once we talked, I realized how much he did mean to me and I thought I should check into the story he and your daughter told me."

"What story?" asked Lorrene, looking sharply from Wren to Adam and Tim.

Sam caught her hand in his and told her in as few words as possible. "I haven't had a chance to tell you; but that's why Wren has been so worried about Tim. She tried to get Mr. Landon to believe her for his protection as well as Tim's."

Adam stabbed his fingers through his dark hair. "I am sorry that it took me so long to listen, Wren. I should've known you weren't playing a game."

108

"Wren is very serious about her detective work," said Sam.

Lorrene sighed heavily. "She certainly is."

"I understand that, now," said Adam.

"We came to get help," said Tim.

Wren's eyes sparkled. "What can we do?"

"Adam has a plan." Tim smiled proudly at Adam. "Don't you?"

Adam nodded. "But I'll need help with it."

"I'll do anything," said Wren.

"Wait a minute," said Lorrene. "I want to hear the plan before we let anyone do anything."

"What do you have in mind?" asked Sam.

Adam took a deep breath and started talking. Wren's eyes sparkled with excitement as she listened, barely able to sit still.

Tim caught her eye and smiled.

She smiled back, feeling his excitement as much as her own.

13

THE TRAP

Monday after school, outside the Landon Building, Wren took a deep breath. "Are we ready?" She looked over at Tim, then back at Bess and Paula.

"Ready," said Tim.

"I don't know if I should do this," said Bess.

"I can't believe you talked me into this, Bird House," said Paula.

The glass door opened and a woman walked out, her purse swinging in her hand. Wren watched until she was all the way down the steps and on the sidewalk. Before she could say anything back to Paula, Tim did.

"If you don't want to help, then go home," said Tim, scowling at Paula.

Paula just glared at Tim, flipped back her hair, pushed past Wren, and walked into the lobby of the Landon Building. It was almost quitting time and there were businessmen and women hurrying to finish for the day.

"Are you sure this will work?" asked Bess, hanging back

with Wren.

"It'll work," Wren said but she didn't know if she felt as sure as she sounded.

Tim jabbed Wren, and hissed, "Look! There's Humphrey up there!"

Wren looked up to see Humphrey standing beside the inner railing in deep conversation with Janice. Fear pricked at her. "Don't let him see us yet."

"Adam said to use the stairs," said Tim. "We can stay out of sight that way."

They all ran toward the stairs.

As Wren walked up with the others, she thought about the plan Adam had devised yesterday afternoon at her house. She was glad that Mom and Dad had agreed to it. She grinned as she thought of Adam's persuasive speech that had finally swayed Mom to his side. Now, if everything went as planned, Humphrey would be caught in his own trap.

At the top floor Wren glanced at her watch. Zero hour was here. Butterflies fluttered in her stomach, but her eyes sparkled with excitement. "It's time," she whispered.

"I'm scared," said Bess.

"If everything goes as planned, you'll be safe," said Tim.

Bess swallowed hard. "What do you mean if?"

Paula tugged her sweater down over her jeans. "He means that this whole thing can fail and we'll all be trapped again and maybe killed."

"Oh, no!" cried Bess, shivering.

"We won't get trapped or killed or hurt," said Wren. "Trust me, will you?"

"Let's stop talking and get going," said Tim.

Wren led the way down the hall, walking quietly on the carpet. She saw Humphrey and Janice still talking. She smiled. This was going to be easier than she'd thought. With a quick wave of her hand she motioned the others onward. Laughter floated to her from a side hallway.

Just then Humphrey looked toward her. A shiver ran down her spine and she quickly ducked out of sight at a corner. "He saw us!"

"Oh, my," said Bess.

"I want to go home," said Paula.

"It's too late now," said Tim. "Come on. This way!"

"No! This way!" Wren grabbed Tim's shirt sleeve and pulled him to a stop. "We'll hide down there!" She pointed to a room with a sticker on the door that said "Plan To Win."

Tim looked and nodded, his face white.

Wren dashed to the door. Was she right? Could they hide here and be safe?

"Hurry!" cried Paula. "He's coming."

"Janice is with him." Tim's voice cracked and he cleared his throat.

Wren turned the knob, but nothing happened. Her

eyes grew big and round and her heart thudded painfully against her rib cage.

"Open it," said Tim.

"Hurry up," said Bess, pushing against Wren.

Wren tried again and this time the knob turned; she dashed inside. Bess almost knocked her over in her rush to escape Humphrey. Tim slammed the door shut and leaned against it, breathing hard.

Wren looked quickly around the room. It was the same size as the one Janice had locked them in before with the same type of table and chairs. But sun shone through a window on the far wall of this room. Pictures and a mirror hung on the other walls. Wren ran to the window and looked down at the street below. Cars crawled past and people walked along the sidewalk.

Just then the doorknob turned and slowly the door opened. Bess squealed, then slapped her hand over her mouth. Paula gasped and fell back a step. Wren ran to Tim's side and waited without breathing.

Humphrey stepped into the room with Janice behind him. His eyes gleamed and he smelled of cigar smoke. Janice's face was dark with anger as she pushed the door shut with a sharp bang and stood against it.

"So, you kids thought you could come and make trouble for me again, did you?" Humphrey flipped back his suit coat and stood with his hands on his hips. "That wasn't very smart of you."

"Let us out and we'll never bother you again," said Wren.

"I want to go home," whispered Bess.

"Why did you come?" asked Janice. She moved and the smell of her cologne drifted out from her and stung Wren's nose.

Wren lifted her chin defiantly. "We decided to try once again to convince Mr. Landon that you're out to steal a client from him."

Humphrey tipped back his dark head and laughed a great bark of a laugh. "He'll never believe you. I saw to that."

"We told him what you did to us," said Tim.

Janice fingered her necklace and looked worried. "Let's get out of here, Geoff. I don't like this."

He frowned at her. "We aren't going to let four little kids ruin our plans, are we?"

"What if Mr. Landon is still here? He could catch us with them and he'd get very suspicious."

"He sure would!" cried Paula. "He'd know we told the truth. I can't understand why he didn't already believe us. My dad's a doctor, you know."

Humphrey rattled the change in his pockets as he studied first Wren and then the others. "I want your names and addresses and then if you ever step foot in this building again, I'll call the security guard to have him hold you until your parents can come. I'll sue your families for everything I can."

"You won't do that," said Wren.

"Won't I, little girl? Watch and see."

"We won't give you our names," said Bess. Her cheeks were flushed a bright pink and her voice quivered, but for once she didn't try to hide behind Wren. "We'll lock our lips shut and not open them." To prove her point she pressed her lips tightly together and didn't say another word.

"And we're going to march right into Mr. Landon's office and tell him the truth about you, and this time he'll believe us," said Wren. She shot a look around. Shivers ran up and down her spine.

Humphrey leaned down toward her, and she smelled his cigar breath. "You are not going anywhere right now. You don't seem to understand that nothing you can say will convince Adam Landon that you're telling the truth."

"Only because you went back to the room that you locked us in Friday and put it in order so that it wouldn't look like anyone had been there," said Wren with her fists doubled at her sides.

Humphrey laughed. "We couldn't let him know that we'd kept you there, could we?"

"You got just what you deserved," snapped Janice. "I told you to leave and you wouldn't."

Tim stepped forward with his head high. "I'll call Sid Ayers and tell him not to go with you when you leave

116

Landon Agency. I'll tell him that you're a crook!"

"He already knows it." Humphrey laughed. "That's what he likes about me. He wants me to sell his furniture any way that I can."

"I don't think he really wants you to steal him from Mr. Landon," said Wren.

"He's a businessman and he likes money," said Humphrey.

"Stop talking and get these kids out of here," said Janice. "I'm getting very nervous."

"You should be," said Tim. "You'll lose your job when Adam Landon finds out that you helped Humphrey."

Wren pointed at Janice. "Are you going to erase Sid's file from the computer? Or maybe change the date on the contract so that it looks like his time is up with Mr. Landon?"

"You're too smart for your own good," snapped Janice.

Humphrey walked across the room and looked out the window, then turned back, his face set. "You kids are staying right here in this room until you tell us your names and addresses."

Wren backed against the table and folded her arms. "I won't tell my name! And the others won't either! You can't make us. You can't get by with stealing from Mr. Landon."

"I already got by with it," snapped Humphrey. "Janice already fixed Sid Ayers' file and contract. As of today, he is my client."

The door opened and Adam Landon walked in with Sam and Lorrene House behind him. Wren was never so glad to see anyone in all of her life. Adam stopped just inches from Humphrey and Janice. "I think we've heard enough."

Humphrey gasped and Janice ran toward the hall door to escape, but Sam easily beat her to the door and blocked her way.

Wren leaped high and shouted, "It worked! The trap worked!"

"For awhile I thought we had the wrong room," said Tim.

"So did I," said Wren.

"You all did a wonderful job," said Lorrene.

"Thanks," said Paula. Bess tried to speak, but couldn't. She leaned weakly against the table and watched the others.

"You're never working in this town again, Geoff," said Adam. "Nor you, Janice."

"You can't stop us," snapped Humphrey.

Lorrene stepped forward. "Holding the children against their will is a crime, Mr. Humphrey. I can see that you spend the next few years in jail."

"I'll call Mick and tell him to come make the arrest," said Sam.

Adam turned to the children. "Thank you for your help. You're brave kids and you helped me. I talked to Sid Ayers this afternoon and convinced him that it was better for his company if he stuck with someone who would handle his campaigns with honesty. He finally agreed."

"Great," said Wren.

"I want to go to the police station and watch them lock up these two," said Tim.

"I think you children have had enough excitement for one day," said Lorrene. "Run on home. Wren, we'll see you there later."

Wren nodded. She turned to Tim and the girls. "Come to my house and we'll talk and have ice cream cones."

Reluctantly Wren walked away from the excitement and led the way to the elevator. As soon as she could, she'd call Amos Pike and tell him every exciting detail.

14

HAPPY AGAIN

Tim stood with his back against the picnic table in Wren's backyard. He looked ready to run away. A tiny smear of chocolate ice cream from the cone he'd just finished marked his chin between freckles.

"Are you going to tell us, or not?" asked Paula.

"You don't have to, Tim," said Wren. A leaf blew across her foot.

"Yes, you do!" cried Bess. "You said if we helped trap Humphrey, you'd tell us who your dad is. I want to know."

Tim cleared his throat. "Adam."

"Adam what?" asked Paula with a frown.

"Adam Landon is my dad," said Tim in a voice just above a whisper.

Bess gasped. "What?"

"Your dad is Adam Landon?" Paula sank to the grass as if her legs had given way. "But that means your dad is richer than my dad."

"Why didn't you know before this?" asked Bess.

"Mom said she didn't want me to know. She said I might want to go live with Adam if I knew."

"Are you going to?" asked Wren.

"I stayed with him over the weekend. That's why I couldn't call you, Wren."

"And I thought Humphrey had kidnapped you." Wren laughed. "I'm glad he didn't."

"Me, too. Being with Adam for the weekend was strange enough. It felt funny with his wife and little girl there. They were nice to me, but I didn't fit in."

"Does he have a maid and a butler?" asked Paula.

"A housekeeper and a maid, but no butler."

Paula flipped back her hair. "If I was that rich, I'd have a butler."

After talking a few more minutes, Bess and Paula ran to their houses. Wren walked Tim to his bike.

"What will you do now, Tim?"

He rubbed his forehead. "Adam talked Mom into going to a clinic to help her stop drinking."

"How'd he convince her?"

Tim swallowed hard. "He told her that if she didn't, he'd take me away from her and she'd never see me again."

Wren shivered. "Oh."

"I'm going to stay with Adam until she gets out."

"And then?"

"Live with Mom."

"Why didn't Adam do something to help your mom

before this?"

"He tried, but he couldn't force her to do anything because his wife and daughter didn't know about me. They thought he was my Big Brother the same as I did."

"Oh."

"Wren, I'm glad you helped me. I'm glad we prayed and God answered."

"Me, too." Wren absently rubbed the handlebar on Tim's bike. "How old is Adam's daughter?"

"She's three." Tim sighed unsteadily. "Her name is Bethany and she likes me, I think."

"That's good. What about Mrs. Landon?"

"She's nice, but she didn't say much to me. She did say that I was welcome there any time I wanted to come. She bought these clothes for me. " He tugged on his sweater and ran a hand down his jeans.

"I'm glad your mom's getting help."

"Me, too. But I'll miss her while she's gone."

Wren nodded. She couldn't imagine being without her mom.

"I've got to go now, Wren."

She nodded and smiled.

"And Wren?"

"Yes?"

"I don't think I want another mystery for awhile. It's just not as much fun when it's about myself."

Wren grinned. "Maybe you're right. But I don't know

if I can live without a mystery."

Tim laughed. "I don't think you can. See you in school tomorrow."

"See you." Wren watched Tim pedal away, then she walked inside and stopped in the kitchen for a banana. Carin and Neil sat at the table drinking orange juice. Wren bit back a surprised gasp.

"Hi, Wren," said Carin with a smile. She was one of the prettiest girls in eighth grade and she was also one of the smartest, almost as smart as Neil.

"Hi." Wren stood uneasily beside the counter. Should she call Bess to tell her that Carin was sitting in their kitchen with Neil? "Are you working on an assignment together?"

"No," said Neil.

Wren's heart sank. Poor Bess.

"Neil's teaching me how to run a computer," said Carin. "I wanted to learn and he said he'd teach me."

Wren's eyes lit up. "Oh, teaching you computer! That's great."

"I think so, but my boyfriend has been a little jealous."

Neil flushed beet red and choked on his drink. "Jealous? Why?"

"That's what I asked him." Carin brushed back her dark hair. "He should know he can trust me. I think you're a nice boy, Neil, but we both know you're more interested in computers than in girls."

"Right," said Neil.

"He is," said Wren. She could barely stand still. "I've got to go see Bess. See you later, Neil. Bye, Carin."

A few minutes later Wren faced Bess at her back door.

"What're you doing here, Wren?"

"I thought you were over being mad at me, Bess."

"Well, I'm not." Wren moved restlessly. She heard music from inside the house. "Can we talk?

Bess hesitated. "I guess so." She led the way to her bedroom. She stood beside her desk and faced Wren. "Well? Talk."

Wren twisted a strand of dark hair around and around her finger. "I don't want you to be mad at me, Bess. I thought you knew I was spending time with Tim to help him."

"You never have time for me."

"Yes, I do. That's why I'm here."

Bess looked down at her blue carpet. "I don't want Paula for a best friend."

"You don't? I'm glad! I want you for my best friend, Bess."

"You do? Really? Not Tim?"

"No, not Tim."

Bess thought about that for a long time, then smiled. "Are we best friends again?"

Wren nodded.

"Good. Will you forgive me for being so bad?"

Wren nodded. She knew that Jesus wanted her to forgive Bess no matter what.

"Good. Now, maybe you can help me with Neil."

Wren sat on the edge of the chair. "That's why I came."

"It is?"

"Carin is at our house right now."

Bess sank to the edge of the bed, her face white. "She is?"

"But she's there to learn computer from Neil. She already has a boyfriend. I asked her."

"Are you sure she doesn't like Neil?"

"Positive."

Bess leaped up with a shout. "I can live again! Let's go to your house right now. Maybe Neil will smile at me, or say hello."

"I have to tell you about Brian, too."

"What about him?"

"It was great, Bess!"

They walked out the back door and headed for Wren's house. "What about Brian?"

"He talked to me in school Friday morning."

Bess squealed. "What did he say?"

Wren told Bess every detail. "I think he likes me, Bess."

"That's awesome!"

Just then Wren saw someone dash down Paula's front steps and race down the sidewalk. "Hold it, Bess."

"What?"